Toni Mount

The Colour of Betrayal

The Colour of Betrayal

A Sebastian Foxley Medieval Mystery
Book 4

Copyright © 2017 Toni Mount
ISBN-13: 978-84-947298-1-2

M
MadeGlobal Publishing

For more information on
MadeGlobal Publishing, visit
our website
www.madeglobal.com

Dedication

To Deborah and Rebecca

Why not visit
Sebastian Foxley's web page
to discover more about his
life and times?
www.SebastianFoxley.com

Prologue

THEY FOUND him in the church, sitting in the vestry. Candles burned, a brazier glowed. The remains of a meal were upon a bench and comfortable bedding lay folded. There was even a fine, plump pillow to aid his rest. How dare he still be fit and able and so well cosseted after what he had done? It was an affront to the Almighty but they would set matters aright; make the miscreant pay for his crime.

Upon seeing three men of authority entering the vestry, the fellow stood up, uncertain as to why they had come. He had followed the correct procedure for claiming the right of sanctuary, so he thought. Perhaps they had come to discuss the finer points of the matter? But if so, then why were they here with a band of ruffians at their backs?

In one swift movement they took hold of him. He was dragged from the cosy vestry, thrown onto the tiled floor of the nave and held down by the weight of many men while a makeshift noose of strips torn from an old linen sheet was put over his head and around his neck. He tried to fight them off but so many pairs of hands, with the strength of so much righteous anger, were more than he could resist unaided. A woman's voice urged them on.

When he attempted to cry out for help, they pulled the linen tighter around his throat, choking his efforts into silent protest. They tied his hands behind him and dragged him beneath a roof beam. A rope was thrown over the beam and the other end was attached to the length of linen about his neck. It took a dozen of them to haul him up, writhing and squirming like a fish on a hook but justice would be served – they would have it no other way. They watched as he died, seeing the frantic light extinguished from his eyes. Then they set to, rearranging the scene, climbing a ladder in order to tie off the end of the linen to the beam and release the dead man's hands from their binding behind his back so they swung limp at his side, all the while unaware of one who watched from a place of concealment, crouched behind the font.

Chapter 1

The eve of Christ's Mass in the year of Our Lord 1476.

SEBASTIAN FOXLEY, his wife, Emily, and their little household were barely recovered from recent events, in particular the hastening into exile of their well-liked journeyman, Gabriel Widowson. He had certainly left a hole in their lives, as well as an empty desk in the stationer's workshop, but business had to continue. In which case, despite the festive season, Seb was in need of a supply of gold leaf before beginning a new commission – a lavishly illuminated copy of Sir Thomas Malory's stories of King Arthur and his Knights of the Round Table. Such a work was an arduous undertaking but, having received an advance of no less than forty marks from Lord Howard, Seb was looking forward to getting to grips with Arthur, Lancelot, Gawain and the other heroes of his childhood in the New Year. First things first – he would need gold leaf for the miniatures, since that had to be applied before any pigments were painted on, and the finest leaf took time to be hammered out of Venetian gold ducats. And who better to supply his needs than a skilled goldsmith and old friend with a most appropriate name: Lawrence Ducket?

After an early fish-day dinner of eels in parsley sauce – it being the eve of a feast day, the Church demanded fasting fare be eaten, even though it was a Tuesday – Seb walked from his house in Paternoster Row. Cheapside was bustling with housewives buying a few last minute items to grace their Christmastide tables, everything from fine diaper table linens to bunches of rosehips, hawthorn and holly berries for those unable or too busy to gather nature's jewels for themselves to brighten their doorways. A juggler and his accompanying hurdy-gurdy man had drawn a crowd that quite blocked the way. Seb managed to squeeze through and turned down Cordwainer Street beside the church of St Mary-le-Bow, into somewhat less crowded waters though just as noisy. Lawrence and his wife, Marjory, lived in a well-appointed house of three storeys which backed onto Soper Lane. Its jettied upper levels gave it an imposing presence that dwarfed the dwellings on either hand and made it seem as though the house itself was frowning in concentration, trying to peer into the windows of its neighbours across the way. Fortunately, the building belied the nature of its owner, for the most part, at least.

Lawrence Ducket greeted his unexpected guest with a smile as wide as his considerable girth.

'Seb Foxley. Welcome, welcome. The felicitations of the season be unto you and yours.'

'And also to you and yours, Lawrence. Are you and Marjory in good health?' Seb asked, enfolded into the goldsmith's embrace, like a sapling in the arms of a bear, grimacing as his ribs were tender still.

'Indeed, my young friend, except for the inconvenient infirmities thrown upon us by the advance of age we are in fine spirits and looking forward to the forthcoming festivities. You and your goodwife are more than welcome to join us, if you will, and that ne'er-do-well brother of yours.' Lawrence's great heaving belly of a laugh took the sting out of his words. 'Still drinking the taverns dry is he?'

'Happily, Jude seems to be a changed man of late,' Seb said, 'He has found love a few weeks since.'

'Truly? Well, we must be living still in an age of miracles, after all. Does this wondrous love have a name?'

'Rose Glover. She lives with us at Paternoster Row now.'

'Consider her invited also. I should like to meet one who works magic.'

'Lawrence? I hear voices: do we have guests? Why have you not asked me for extra cups and ale?' A rotund little apple of a woman bustled into the passage from the kitchen, wiping floury hands upon her apron. 'You haven't even invited him into the parlour, Lawrence. Where be your manners? Ah, Sebastian, 'tis you. What a joyous occurrence.'

'Aye, but I doubt he's come for any purpose but business, Marjory,' Lawrence said.

Seb greeted Marjory with a kiss on her cheek.

'Greetings, Mistress Marjory, God give you good day.'

'And you also, Sebastian. How is young Emily and Jude and all of you? 'Tis too long since we last saw you and we heard of your mishap in saving that lad's life on the church roof. Such goings-on had us quite concerned.'

'Nonsense, wife. I saw him last month. That be often enough.' Lawrence's laughter bubbled over like a boiling pottage pot. 'But I would hear of your adventure.'

'Shall I serve ale or wine?' Marjory asked.

'Neither, woman. You have enough to do in that kitchen in preparation for the morrow. Don't forget we have important guests to feed and entertain. Seb and I will go to the Green Man for our refreshment, to discuss business without disturbing you.'

The tavern at the sign of the Green Man was busy indeed. It seemed a good many folk were determined that the celebration of the birth of Our Lord, Jesu Christ should begin early. Seb

5

shook his head, wondering at so many drunken sots afore midday. What would they be like by the time they should attend the Midnight Vigil and Christ's Mass? If they got there at all.

'Make way! Make way!' Lawrence bellowed above the din of revelry, 'Thirsty men coming through. Ah, landlord, a large jug of best Gascon wine, if you please?'

'Thank you, Lawrence, but a cup of ale will suffice for me,' Seb put in hastily.

'Nonsense, lad, 'tis good wine for us at Christmastide. I'll settle the reckoning, never fear, knowing a poor scrivener like you has to guard every penny.' Again, the goldsmith's good humour made it impossible to take offence.

Once seated – Lawrence having booted a couple of youngsters off a bench by the hearth – they were served by the tavern-keeper in person. An obsequious little man, he grovelled unashamedly before the wealthy goldsmith:

'Sir Lawrence, welcome as ever, good sir. Anything you need, you have but to ask and it shall be done.'

'Spare me your toadying, Barnabas, it makes me quite queasy. I be certain you have other customers aplenty whom you could annoy instead. Be gone.' Lawrence filled both cups almost to the brim and took a hefty swallow from his own. 'Now, Seb, what business brought you to my door this day?'

'I simply wished to place an order for gold leaf, ready for the New Year. I have a new commission to fulfil.'

'Another royal patron, perchance?'

'Not quite. Lord Howard has...'

'Ah. John Howard. A good fellow, indeed. Purchased some fine pieces of jewellery from me a week since. Said they were a New Year gift for his lady but, noting the twinkle in his eye as he spoke, I doubt he meant his wife. Still, the morals of the high born are no concern of mine. However...' Lawrence indicated with the jug before refilling his cup. '...Men of the cloth are another matter entirely. See that scurrilous-looking dandified fool garbed like a mountebank? The one wearing that hideous chaperon in a ghastly shade of piss yellow?'

'Aye. I see him.' Seb winced at Lawrence's description of the colour of the man's hat but he wasn't far wrong. It was a most unsavoury hue even in the gloom of the tavern. 'What of him, Lawrence?' Seb shook his head as his friend was about to top up his cup. 'Nay, I thank you but my cup be still full.'

'Well, drink up then. I tell you, Seb, that fellow, with no more meat upon him than a yard of string, is a cleric. Prinked up in his finery, he's the Town Clerk of London. Despite being in holy orders, I assure you, my friend, that woman sitting beside him is neither mother nor sister nor niece to him. See how he fondles her in full view? It quite disgusts me. The authorities ought to put a stop to it, except for the inconvenient and unpalatable fact that he *is* the authority in this city. Ralph Aldgate is the wretch's name and I be of a mind to tell him exactly what I think of his carrying on with that harlot of his.'

'Hush, Lawrence, I beg you. Now is not the time. Please.' Seb put his hand on the goldsmith's arm. 'Forebear for Marjory's sake.'

'Mm. You be right, Seb. Here and now is neither the place nor the hour. I'll wait a while but, I warn you, I have never liked him, though he be a neighbour. God rot him but his kind ruin the reputation of Cordwainer Street Ward. It used to be a respectable ward until he moved in, lowering the reputation of us all. I needs must teach him a lesson.' The goldsmith made to rise from the bench but Seb held on to the squirrel-fur trim of his cloak.

'Not now. A week hence maybe. When you have consumed rather less wine.'

'Are you accusing me of being drunk, young Foxley? Because if you are...'

'No, Lawrence, I accuse you of no such thing,' Seb said, trying to soothe his friend's humour, 'But 'tis the season of good will to *all men*, is it not? Should that not include Ralph Aldgate too?'

'Aye, I suppose so, though it grieves me to bear good will to his sort and that whore of his.'

'Shh. Have pity, my friend. Come, let me see you home to Marjory.'

'Certainly not. I paid for this wine and it must not go to waste. We shall finish the jug, first.'

'No, Lawrence. Emily would never forgive me if I attend mass this eve with my wits addled. I am singing an anthem in St Paul's and must be sober for that.'

'But wine improves the singing voice... 'tis a proven fact, lad.'

'For others it might, but not for me.'

The wine jug was empty at last and Seb refused Barnabas' pleading that he should be permitted to replenish it. Cajoling and guiding Lawrence by turns, he succeeded in getting the goldsmith outside the tavern. The latter was somewhat uncertain upon his feet. It was as well his house was but a matter of a hundred yards or so away. Seb couldn't support a fellow twice as heavy as himself any farther.

How unfortunate it was that Ralph Aldgate chose the same moment to leave the Green Man with the woman on his arm.

'Alice, my lamb, you won't forget, will you? You did promise me, concerning the festivities upon the morrow,' Ralph was saying.

'Forget you, Ralph? Indeed, I shall not.' Alice At-Bowe giggled like a silly maid. 'You are unforgettable, my stallion.'

'Hey! You, there, you mangy dog!' Lawrence bawled from across the street, shrugging himself free of Seb's supporting arm. 'You devil's spawn. How dare you bring our respectable neighbourhood into such ill-repute, consorting so openly with that wanton harlot? Look at her! Wearing that fancy henin so far above her station. Who does she think she is?'

'Hush, my friend,' Seb urged, attempting to pull Lawrence homeward. 'Do not make a scene in a public place.'

'I'll do as I wish. This scurvy knave must be taken to task for his disgraceful behaviour.' Lawrence brushed Seb's restraining hand from his arm and crossed the gutter. 'I be addressing you, Ralph Aldgate!' he shouted. 'You and your whore.' The goldsmith, clumsy in his drunken state, made a grab for the cleric but missed, catching the fur of the woman's green cloak instead and dragging her into the middle of the street.

She screamed and her escort turned on Lawrence and shoved him away.

'Unhand my lady, you brute,' Ralph snarled.

'She's no lady. She's a slut, a brothel-keeper's bitch.'

Ralph's puny fist caught Lawrence on the shoulder, doing him no hurt whatever but it was enough for the goldsmith to lose his temper utterly.

'Don't touch me, you worm-riddled cur,' Lawrence yelled and struck the skinny cleric with all the force he could muster, full in the face. Blood spurted, splashing both the cleric's handsome doublet and the goldsmith's cloak. Ralph Aldgate fell backwards, like a tree beneath a forester's axe, and, for good measure, his head smote the stone, used as a mounting block beside the door of the Green Man tavern. He neither groaned nor twitched but lay corpse-still. His chaperon hat lay in the gutter.

'Ralph! Ralph!' Alice screamed, going on her knees in the mud to tend her paramour. 'You've killed him, you murderous devil. You'll pay for this, Lawrence Ducket.'

Seb also knelt to see how the man fared, feeling for the pulse in his neck, relieved to find it was still there, though beating feebly.

9

'Nay, mistress, he yet lives. You, lad, in the brown worsted.' Seb singled out a likely looking youngster from the little crowd that had swiftly gathered to gawp at the spectacle. A spillage of blood never failed to attract onlookers and, in this case, the spillage was considerable as the pool of gore beneath the injured man's was ever spreading. 'Run to Surgeon Dagvyle's place. You know it? 'Tis but around the corner in Ironmonger Lane. Tell him Seb Foxley sent you; he knows me well enough. Take this for your trouble.' He pressed a half groat into the lad's hand. 'Go. Hasten!'

'What have I done, Sebastian?' Lawrence groaned, suddenly sober. 'God knows I never meant to kill him.' He buried his face in his hands.

'You don't know your own strength, my friend, but in this case, thankfully, the fellow lives still.' Seb patted the goldsmith's shoulder. 'And, God willing, he will recover.'

'How can that be? See how the wretch bleeds. He is dying; I know, and at my hand. I'm a murderer. What will become of me? Of my poor dear Marjory?'

'Do not despair, Lawrence. Surgeon Dagvyle knows his craft. When my ribs were broke this last month past, he had me bound up like a babe in swaddling and I made a fair recovery, as you see. If this fellow can be saved, Dagvyle will do it.'

Alice stood up. Her sleeves were covered in blood and tears coursed down her cheeks.

'I'm raising the hue and cry!' she cried, 'Take that felon in hand.' She pointed a gory finger straight at Lawrence.

'Oh, Seb. What shall I do?' the goldsmith whimpered, seeming to shrink into himself.

Seb thought quickly.

'Claim sanctuary, Lawrence. St Mary's holds that right. Now, run.'

'You think?'

'Aye. There be no time to consider.'

Lawrence bolted into the church of St Mary-le-Bow across the way.

'Sanctuary! I claim sanctuary in the name of the Blessed Trinity,' he shouted as he dashed through the west door and up the nave. He did not hesitate at the archway through the rood screen but entered the chancel – the domain of priests – and flung himself at the altar, grabbing a handful of the hem of the cloth that draped the sacred table. 'I claim sanctuary,' he sobbed, kissing the cloth. 'Spare me. I never meant to kill...' Lawrence's words tailed off as he lay prostrate upon the altar step, lamenting this sudden turn of ill-fortune.

The band of spectators that had watched the event now became, perforce, the hue and cry, pursuing their quarry to apprehend him. But espying him, lying upon the chancel floor, the corner of the altar cloth clutched in his desperate hands, they would not pass beyond the rood screen to take him.

'We must send for the authorities. Summon the sheriffs,' someone said. Voices muttered agreement; heads nodded. No one would dare violate sanctuary once the right had been exercised so they left Lawrence Ducket to suffer his misery alone. Even Simon Thornbury, the priest of St Mary's was uncertain what was to be done next. Being fairly new to this incumbency, he had never had anyone claim sanctuary before. He must consult with Bishop Kemp on the matter, in order to learn how best to proceed. In the meantime, the fellow attempting to flee justice would be ignored, at least by the priest.

Outside on the street, Seb waited with Alice At-Bowe, her elaborate headdress all askew, for Surgeon Dagvyle's arrival to attend the injured cleric. As time passed, the medical man failed to appear and Alice verged upon the brink of hysteria. Seb realised the lad to whom he had paid the half groat was likely spending it in some tavern or other, rather than bothering to fetch assistance from Ironmonger Lane. He didn't want to abandon the woman in her distress, nor would he trust another passer-by to summon the surgeon. Torn betwixt staying at the scene or going to Ironmonger Lane himself, he was relieved when Surgeon Dagvyle came wheezing along, escorted by the lad. So pleased was Seb to discover his judgement had not gone awry in the choice of a messenger, he gave the lad another penny for his efforts.

John Dagvyle cursed silently as he eased his portly frame down beside the limp form of Ralph Aldgate. He was getting too old for grovelling on the cold, damp ground in this manner but at least there were no stairs to climb – the bane of his life. A cart rumbled past and Seb stood, holding wide the hem of his mantle, to shield both surgeon and patient from the mud splashed up by the wheels.

'Fetch a hurdle, carry him home,' Dagvyle instructed no one in particular. 'I cannot examine him properly in the midst of the street. For pity's sake, Master Sebastian, help me up won't you?'

Seb obliged before realising that no one else was going to organise the fetching of a hurdle. Sighing, he went knocking on doors, asking if anyone had such a thing that they might spare for a while. Eventually, a kindly woman living in Soper Lane offered her trestle board and an old blanket – for which Seb felt he ought to dip into his purse again and offer another penny. But the woman shook her head, saying it was an act of Christian charity at Christmastide, so long as the board was returned in time for her to serve her goodman's supper upon it. He assured her he would see that it was.

By now, one of the city sheriffs, John Stocker, had arrived, and the beadle for Cordwainer Street Ward, Paul Draper, bringing two burly constables. Beadle Draper ordered his constables to carry Ralph Aldgate home to Budge Row with Alice leading the way and Surgeon Dagvyle following on, puffing and blowing as their course was somewhat up hill. As they walked away, Sheriff Stocker questioned Seb about what had come to pass.

Seb explained in as few words as possible. He was tired, mud-splattered and cold and wanted to go home. Emily would be worried that he had been gone far longer than expected. And then there was the matter of the return of the trestle board, as he'd promised the woman.

'And where is the miscreant?' asked Stocker. 'Did the hue and cry apprehend him?'

'No, sir. Lawrence Ducket has claimed sanctuary in St Mary's, as is his right. The poor fellow fears his crime of assault might become one of murder, if Aldgate should fail to survive.'

'As well may be the case, from what I saw. I don't hold with this sanctuary business. Ralph Aldgate is a friend of mine and deserves justice for this foul attack upon his person. If he dies...' The sheriff left the word dangling like a hangman's noose.

Seb shook his head.

'My friend was angry and somewhat the worse for wine. He never meant to inflict a hurt so severe. It was a terrible accident made worse when Aldgate struck his head upon the mounting stone. A bloody nose may have been intended but no worse, I swear.'

'Aye, well we'll see about that,' Stocker said, sounding ominous, 'Wait until Thomas Rigby hears what has happened to his closest and dearest friend.' He was referring to the longest-serving under-sheriff the city had ever had, a man whose sense of justice sometimes pushed him beyond the precise letter of the law. Yet he was greatly respected by the Lord Mayor and aldermen as a fellow who performed his often thankless tasks with efficiency and little complaint. Officers of the law of Rigby's calibre were rare indeed and therefore precious to the authorities. 'At least, as yet, we don't have to involve that fat fart

Bulman, that idiot calling himself the City Deputy-Coroner.'
Sheriff Stocker made a dismissive gesture, showing his opinion
of Master Bulman.

Back home at last, having waited upon Surgeon Dagvyle's
assessment of his patient's condition and returned the trestle
board to the charitable woman in Soper Lane, Seb was further
wearied by an interrogation concerning his tardiness in returning
for supper.

'How long does it take to order a few leaves of gold, eh?'
Emily stood, hands on hips in the midst of her kitchen. 'Why
we should all go hungry awaiting your presence, I'm at a loss to
know. And you'll be late for your last choir rehearsal before the
Christ's Mass, if you don't get cleaned up right swiftly. Just look
at the state of you and as for your mantle... how did it get so
begrimed? Were you rolling in the mud? I might excuse young
Jack for coming home so filthy but you – a grown man. What
were you thinking? And what is this?' She examined the front
of his jerkin, pulling him towards the candlelight so she could
see better. 'Sweet Jesu! This is blood, Seb. Are you injured? Is it
your ribs broke anew?'

'No, sweetheart. 'Tis blood, aye, but not mine. Fear not,
Em.' He slumped onto the stool at the head of the table board.

Rose, Tom Bowen and Jack Tabor were ready seated. Nessie
stood by, ladle in hand, waiting to serve their supper of a thick
vegetable pottage.

'Shall I pour you some ale, Master Seb?' Rose offered, the new
lodger sounding a good deal more compassionate than his wife.

'Aye, Rose, I would be grateful. The afternoon was quite
fraught indeed. Is there any cheese, Em?'

'There is but that is tomorrow's fare. Are you not content with
fine bread and pottage for an eve of fasting like the rest of us?'

'Not for me, Em. 'Tis for Lawrence Ducket.'

'Giving charity to wealthy goldsmiths now, are we? I'm sure he can afford to eat better than we.'

'You don't understand. I must go to Cordwainer Street to visit Marjory Ducket. As yet she may still be unaware of what has befallen her goodman and, on the way, since I shall pass St Mary's, I can see that Lawrence doesn't go hungry, if you will bundle up some bread and cheese for him, please?'

'Not until you explain yourself. You are speaking in riddles.'

'Forgive me, sweetheart, I am weary but I will tell you. It happened in this manner...'

Slowly, haltingly, with many a detour and omission, Seb told those gathered about the supper board of the tragic happenings outside the Green Man tavern.

'Will the fellow – Aldgate was his name? – be likely to recover?' Emily asked, dipping her bread into her bowl. 'Eat up, Seb, your pottage is going cold.'

'Surgeon Dagvyle is cautiously hopeful but says head injuries be chancy things. It cannot be certain whether it will prove mortal or no for a week at least.' Seb, recalled to his food, finally thought to take up his spoon. 'But he was able to stem the bleeding. As for Lawrence, his forty days of grace in sanctuary should be time enough to learn the true extent of his error: whether it was an action of common assault, or a deed with worse consequences. I have the greater sympathy for his wife. She must suffer also, despite being innocent of any wrong-doing, poor woman.'

'Well, we of this household are innocent too, but you make us suffer anxieties, not knowing where you are or what you be about. Mistress Ducket is not the only one, yet do you spare a grain of sympathy for us, Sebastian Foxley? No. You do not. Being *your* wife deserves sympathy indeed. Have you finished?' Without waiting for reply, Emily removed Seb's bowl from the board in front of him, even though it remained more than half full, and snatched away the spoon from his grasp.

Seb sighed and made do with bread and ale. He was in the wrong, as usual. It served him right for having married a feisty lass, as her father had warned him.

'I like Mistress Ducket,' Jack said.

'Aye, lad, she is a benevolent woman.' Seb chewed on his bread.

'A wot?'

'Benevolent means kindly, Jack.' Seb shook his head. He had learned long since to use simple words when speaking to Jack but, in his weariness, he had forgotten.

'She was benervalent t' me, master, back when I wos 'ard done by.' Jack recalled the uncounted years of his childhood spent mostly as a street urchin, until the Foxleys had taken him in. He had learned to time his visits to the large house in Cordwainer Street to the hour following the wealthy goldsmith's dinner, when Mistress Ducket would espy him from her window and see to it that the skinny little lad got a generous bowlful of the tastiest leftovers in London, as Jack reckoned them. A more shameful incident – one he preferred not to think about too much and had never told a soul – involved Master Ducket. One day, the goldsmith had dropped his bulging purse upon his doorstep and it had burst open, scattering coins on the ground. Jack had seen the mishap and, being more nimble and able to bend as Master Ducket couldn't, he had helped the man to gather up his money. Grateful, the man had pressed two groats – eight pence, no less – into Jack's hand as a reward. It had made him feel somewhat ashamed for the other coins he had already purloined and hidden in his rags.

'I 'ope everyfing turns out well for 'em,' he added.

Master Seb patted him on the head and smiled.

'A worthy sentiment, young Jack,' he said.

Jack didn't bother to ask what a 'senterment' was.

If Seb hastened, there was just time to take the bread and cheese to Lawrence, make a swift visit to Marjorie and get back to St Paul's for choir practice, else the precentor would be in a rage.

Seb found the goldsmith in a sorry case, hunched in the chancel, still clinging to the hem of the altar cloth. The man's eyes were red-rimmed with weeping and he said little that made any sense but kept repeating how sorry he was.

'I brought you some food, my friend,' Seb said, handing him a linen napkin with bread and cheese wrapped within.

'I'm so sorry,' Lawrence moaned. 'Sorry to cause all this trouble. I'm too sorrowful to eat.'

'You have to keep your strength up. Surgeon Dagvyle is quite hopeful of Aldgate's recovery.'

'Did he not see how much blood there was?'

'Head wounds always bleed out of all proportion, Lawrence. Be not disheartened, I beg you. Dagvyle is a good surgeon.'

'He's naught but a charlatan if he tells you he can mend a broken head, one that has been cracked upon a stone.'

'Even so, you but broke his nose. 'Twas the stone that broke his head and you did not put it there by the door, such that Aldgate should strike his head upon it when he fell. An accident is what it was, Lawrence.'

'The law won't see it that way. It will adjudge me a murderer if, or more likely when, he dies. I'm done for, Seb. I must choose betwixt eternal exile from the realm or the gallows. Such is my Christmas gift to Marjory. In which case, the gallows will be best since that will leave her a widow and able to remarry. If I choose exile, then she must wait seven years to have me declared a dead man...'

'Enough, Lawrence. It won't come to that. Aldgate will recover, I'm certain. Now. Do you have a message for Marjory that I may give her? I'm going to your house now, to see that she is not in need of ought that I can provide.'

'You're a good soul, Sebastian. I'm sorry I involved you in my quarrel. My humours were so out of sorts. Just tell Marjory... tell her I'm that sorry... tell her...' The goldsmith dissolved in tears again.

Seb never knew how best to deal with weeping so he simply said, 'I'll light a candle for you both, my friend,' and left St Mary's, choking back tears himself.

Marjory Ducket's plump, rosy-apple cheeks had lost their lustre. Neighbours had told her of her beloved Lawrence's situation within the hour of its occurrence. Then Sheriff Stocker turned up at her door, just as she was donning hood and mantle, about to rush to St Mary's. The sheriff spoke bluntly, forbidding her to visit her goodman, else his claim to sanctuary would be deemed violated and they would arrest him forthwith. Marjory did not know the precise nature of the rights of sanctuary but that did not seem to ring true somehow. But fearful that she might cause Lawrence further trouble, she obeyed Stocker, at least for the present. She would look more deeply into the matter as soon as she might.

Seb knocked at the door of the goldsmith's imposing house, wary that he might be disturbing a distraught woman. Mistress Ducket opened the door herself. Seb could tell straightway that she had been told of events for her cheek was pale, her features drawn with worry, yet she seemed composed as she invited him over the threshold.

'Sebastian. You are a welcome sight indeed,' Marjory said, as she managed a smile and ushered him into the cosy parlour. Flames danced in the hearth, its grand overmantle garlanded with holly and ivy in celebration of the season, bright with red and black berries. Candlelight sparkled on the shiny evergreens but such joyous colours were too garish now, an offence against a day filled with cares. Marjory called out 'Stop snivelling Agnes and bring some hot spiced ale for Master Foxley.'

Seb knew he had no time to spare but he would welcome some warming drink for the evening was turning chill. Besides, it would be discourteous to refuse. He could hardly hasten away without speaking of what had come to pass outside the Green Man earlier.

'I'm so glad you've come, Sebastian,' Marjory said as they settled back into cushioned chairs either side of the fire. 'I've heard such garbled versions from my neighbours and Sheriff Stocker said even less, I hardly know what is true. Please tell me how my Lawrence comes to be in such trouble that he must claim sanctuary.'

Seb retold the story in better fashion this time, having thought it through and related it twice before.

Marjory listened without interruption, seemingly calm and resolute but the glint of tears in her eyes and the twitching of her lips betrayed her anguish.

'Lawrence has always been of a choleric temperament,' she said, sighing, 'I suppose it was bound to happen one day, that his ill-humour would override reason. Poor Lawrence. An over-fondness for Gascon wine has been his weakness ever since I knew him. But what's to be done now, Sebastian? What does the right of sanctuary entail?'

'In truth, mistress, I don't know but I promise to look into it as soon as I may,' Seb said.

'Sheriff Stocker told me I may not even visit Lawrence. How then shall he have food and drink and keep warm? I worry so about him.' Her voice bore the hint of a tremor now and Seb feared her brittle air of composure might be about to shatter. He could not bear to witness yet more tears from anyone.

'Fear not. I shall see to it that he does not go hungry, mistress. I gave him bread and cheese afore I came here but, if you have a blanket or some such to ward off the cold, I could take it to him now, on my way back. I must be at St Paul's shortly.'

He finished his spiced ale, savouring the flavour of cinnamon, cloves, nutmeg and honey while Marjory and the serving maid, Agnes, bustled about, gathering a few necessities to see Lawrence through the night.

'You're a kind soul, Sebastian. I hope I haven't made you late by causing you to wait?' Marjory said. A few necessities amounted to her piling blankets, a cushion and a fur coverlet into his arms and pressing the handle of a basket into his free hand at the front door. Added to his burden now was the necessity of a lighted torch for it was growing dusk. 'Tell Lawrence I'll be praying for him every moment.' At which point she began to sob.

'I will, mistress,' Seb said, hastening into the darkening street. 'May God have you in His care,' he called back. As for being late; it was past time for choir practice already and now he must go by way of St Mary's once again. The precentor was going to be beyond anger, such that God's wrath might be less fearful. But it couldn't be helped. Someone had to see that Lawrence was cared for. Peering around the load he carried – goodness knew what was in the basket that weighed so heavy – Seb returned to St Mary's.

Lawrence was pathetically grateful, as well he might be, since he now had all that was needful to make up a comfortable bed upon the chancel floor and a most extensive night livery of cheeses, cold meats, dried fruits, oat cakes, a pot of butter and another of bramble jelly and a stoppered flask of wine, together with the appropriate platters, napkins, knives, spoons and a cup. Little wonder the basket had proved so heavy. Seb bade him "good night" as swiftly as possible without seeming rude and scurried to St Paul's as fast as his reluctant hip allowed on a night so chill. The goldsmith would not lack company once the parishioners of St Mary's began to arrive for the Midnight Vigil and Christ's Mass.

Seb was right: the precentor was in a towering rage, all his wrath directed at his tardy soloist. So much for the season of good will towards all men. Clearly, that did not include Seb. His attempt to explain was cut short by an explosion of invective, utterly unsuited to a sacred place. At any other time, St Paul's choir master was a pleasant fellow indeed but a man disrupted his choral practices at great peril.

It did not improve matters when a young chorister suffered a fit of sneezing which set his fellows laughing, trying to muffle their mirth with the sleeves of their blue gowns. Then one of the vicars choral – a man with a good bass voice – dropped his song book and knocked over an artful arrangement of evergreens in a copper pot with such a clatter, spilling water down the chancel steps and strewing leaves and dried seed heads across the newly-swept tiled floor. Even the portable organ seemed out of sorts, the bellows wheezing like a beggar with consumption, the loose keys at middle C and A rattling worse than usual, as if its teeth chattered with cold.

With less than an hour to go before Bishop Kemp should bestir himself, in honour of Christ Jesu's birth, to conduct the office in person, Seb had his moment to redeem his reputation with the precentor. His humours felt so unsettled, his palms greasy with sweat though his body was chill. He was shivering and feared this would be evident when he sang, a vibrato in his voice that was not intended.

Seb did what he always did when he sang. He banished all thoughts of the precentor, his fellow choristers and the gasping organ. Earthly troubles were set aside as he gazed upwards, not seeing the gilded roof beams nor star-spangled plasterwork between. Rather, he saw the invisible beyond. He sang so the Heavenly Host and Almighty God Himself might hear his hymn of praise, if they wished. They were his audience as Seb poured his heart into every soaring note, his whole spirit into the quieter cadences and his very soul into the last 'Amen'. Naught else mattered until the echo of that final note had faded into the silent fabric of the cathedral.

Only then did Seb return to mundane concerns, looking around like a night owl blinking in daylight. No one spoke but he could see in their eyes the choristers' admiration and wonder. He had redeemed himself. Not that the precentor would admit as much.

'Aye. I suppose that was a fair enough rendition, Sebastian,' he said. 'The top C of "angeli" could have been held a moment longer, of course, for better effect. They're angels, Sebastian, glorious messengers of God, not kitchen drabs. I trust you'll improve upon it in the bishop's presence?'

'I shall do my best, sir.'

His soloist suitably chastened, the precentor turned back to the rest of the choristers.

'Now, to the final Gloria. That is in desperate need of attention. Feeble. That's what it was last time. You sounded like a herd of braying donkeys with the quinsy.'

And so the choir practice continued. The precentor was a hard task-master but the choristers always strived to impress him and, thus, were ever a credit to St Paul's.

The office of the vigil and the Christ's Mass that followed it had gone well. Seb excelled himself such that even Bishop Kemp had managed an approving nod and – a wonder in itself – the precentor had actually smiled at him.

'I'm so proud of you. That was beautiful indeed, husband,' Emily whispered, taking his arm as others gathered around him in the great candlelit nave to express their pleasure at his success. But it was her few words that Seb had most wanted to hear.

After the office, his brother Jude had come to Paternoster Row to share a cup of ale before returning to his lodgings in Cheapside. Persuading Jude to leave was no easy task. It was well known how smitten he was with Rose and Emily had hung a mistletoe bough above the parlour door. Having discovered it, Jude made full use of it, kissing Rose long and lustily.

'Hold off, brother,' Seb laughed, 'Leave a few kissing berries for the rest of us. I haven't had my due from Em yet.'

'I'm not certain you deserve it anyway,' Emily told him with mock severity, since a smile threatened to curve her lips, 'But you sang right well, so I suppose I may allow just one small...'

Seb needed no further encouragement but dragged his wife beneath the mistletoe, jostling Jude and Rose aside.

'Off to bed, you three,' Emily told Jack, Tom and Nessie as she pulled back from Seb's embrace to catch her breath, 'The hour is late and this is grown-ups' business...' She gave a little squeal that was muffled as Seb resumed his kisses.

Chapter 2

CHRISTMAS MORN dawned bright, glittering with a thick frost. Every church bell in London chimed, pealed and clanged to welcome the Christ Child and celebrate the day. The nave of their little parish church of St Michael-le-Querne was fogged with breath in the cold air at every response made. The braziers burned but fingers and toes were soon numbed with cold yet the mood of the parishioners was so joyous, they hardly noticed. Extra candles shone in the gloom and the rising sun streamed through the east window, casting the jewelled colours of the stained glass across the floor, turning the worn and faded tiles to a vivid Turkey carpet beneath their feet. Evergreen boughs hung from every ledge and decked the font at the back of the little church.

Father Thomas kept his sermon brief, extolling everyone to bear good will to all men and to remember those less fortunate, even as they were sitting down to their feast day dinners. But the priest knew his flock well enough: there were those among them who would think to aid the poor, even without his timely reminder, and those who would never allow such unsavoury matters to cross their minds and spoil a fine repast. In either case, preaching at them served no purpose, so he wouldn't waste the words. As for himself, Father Thomas would be dining with his sister's family in Coleman Street and did not want to be late.

Afterwards, neighbours were wishing each other the joys of the season, exchanging kisses and invitations to share in the festivities. Emily, Rose and Nessie hastened home to continue the preparations for dinner, taking Tom, the elder, more sensible apprentice, with them to do the fetching, carrying and lifting, leaving Seb to invite others to share the meal with the Foxley household. There was going to be quite a crowd. In the meantime, Seb would walk over to Cordwainer Street to see that Mistress Marjory was not alone and sorrowful this day. If she was, she too could join them for dinner.

'Come with me, Jack. 'Tis best that you and that dog of yours stay out of Mistress Em's way this morn,' Seb said. 'Can't have Little Beggar chasing his tail and causing chaos in the kitchen, can we? Nor helping himself to roasted goose, either.'

'Will there be a Christmas Pie, like last year, master? I liked that the best.' Jack was skipping down Cheapside beside Seb, merry as a monkey, with Beggar nosing into every new scent along the way, tail a-wagging. And there were so many smells, apart from the usual stink of horse dung, cess pits, pigs and wood fires. Spicy aromas wandered from open windows to tickle noses. All kinds of meats roasting on spits sent enticing hints of deliciousness into the chill airs of London. Jack's mouth was watering already with hours still to go until dinner. 'And can I 'ave the first spoonful from the pie t' make a wish, agen, like las' time?'

'I don't know, Jack. The first helping always goes to the youngest and that isn't you this year.'

'But I am the youngest,' Jack insisted, 'Apart from Beggar, an' he don't know 'ow t' make a wish.'

'You are forgetting: Dick and Bella Langton are coming from Deptford, bringing their little lass, Janie, who is but one year of age. For certain, she is the youngest. I'm sorry, Jack. No wishes for you.'

THE COLOUR OF BETRAYAL

'But she's a babe,' Jack protested. 'She won't know what t' wish for, will she?'

'Well, Dick says she's very forward for her age, so mayhap she will be quite capable of wishing for a velvet robe, or a diamond pendant.'

As they turned into Cordwainer Street, Jack, his bottom lip protruding like a storeroom shelf, caught sight of his master's face. Master Seb was biting his cheek to keep from laughing, his grey eyes twinkling.

'You be joshing me! That's not fair, master.' Jack stamped his foot.

'Forgive me, lad,' Seb said, chuckling, 'Your face was such an image of dejection, I couldn't resist the temptation.'

'Wot's derjecton mean, then?'

'It means we are going to have a wonderful meal and, most certainly, you shall have the first helping of pie. Now, catch Beggar's halter and behave yourself in Mistress Ducket's presence, particularly if we be invited in. You'll have to tether him securely to the post.'

As the serving maid, Agnes, opened the door, Seb realised he need have no fear of Marjory Ducket passing a lonely Christmas. The passage was full of children, from toddlers tottering to those around Jack's age in full flight, all in a boisterous game of Hoodman Blind.

'Come in, Sebastian. Join us in the parlour,' Mistress Marjory called out. 'I'm sure Bedlam was never so noisy. Ah, Jack. How do you fare, little master?'

Jack seemed to grow by a hand's span, being addressed so. He made his bow and spoke up.

'I do right well, Mistress Ducket, fanking you.'

'Such a courteous lad deserves a treat, if Master Sebastian permits?'

Seb nodded and grinned.

The heaped dish of sweetmeats that Mistress Ducket offered him made Jack's eyes go wide, like one struck upon the head and astounded. Except instead of stars, he saw dried plum suckets dripping with honey and ginger, baked beaten egg-whites and sugar, like frothy mounds of snow turned golden at the edges, sprinkled with cinnamon and chopped blanched almonds, and marchpane circles, decorated with gold leaf. Mistress Ducket called them angels' haloes. Spoilt for choice, Jack's fingers hovered over the dish.

'Take one of each. Then you can join my nieces and nephews in their game.'

By the time Marjory had introduced Seb to her elderly uncle, her brother- and sister-by-marriage, her widowed sister and two cousins, and served him mulled ale and wafers, the morning was passing. The children's game had long since spilled out, onto the street, where neighbours joined the fun. Marjory led Seb into the kitchen where the womenfolk were putting the final touches to the feast day food. The merry smile was gone from her face, as though a dark cloud had suddenly covered the sun.

'I've put some meats and a few choice bits and pieces in this basket for my poor Lawrence,' she said softly, so Seb alone should hear. 'Would you play the Good Samaritan, Sebastian, and take it to St Mary's for me, please? I cannot go myself. I've told everyone that Lawrence was called away unexpectedly upon the king's business. It happened thus a few years ago and, I admit, I know not how to tell our guests the truth. I suppose I will have to, but it can wait a day or two. Lawrence is safe for now, at least.'

'Willingly, mistress,' Seb said. 'I think you are wise to delay. And rest assured, I shall see to it that Lawrence has supper this eve also.'

'May God bless you,' she said and kissed his cheek. Only then did Seb realise he was standing beneath a sprig of mistletoe.

Seb delivered the basket, as promised. Lawrence was downcast but relieved to hear that Marjory was coping admirably with their guests despite his absence. Seb and Jack left him with words of good cheer as the goldsmith munched on slices of roasted pork and goose.

Seb was singing a carol and Jack joined in as they knocked at first upon Stephen Appleyard's door, then on Dame Ellen Langton's. Emily's father and younger brother, John, were waiting, ready cloaked, as was Dame Ellen. The elderly woman had been the brothers' landlady at one time and now Jude had moved back to their previous lodgings. The good dame was also Emily's employer as a silkwoman. Jude was ready too, wearing his best doublet and favoured red boots, wanting to impress Rose, of course. John Appleyard was pushing a handcart laden with an extra board and trestle, two benches and a couple of stools, needed to seat so many diners. Dame Ellen added a selection of cushions, so all could be comfortable, a pristine tablecloth and spare napkins and a covered dish of her famous almond wafers. Jude's contribution was a large bunch of mistletoe – Seb had no doubt of his brother's reason for bringing that – and a jug of Gascon wine.

The beggar, known as Old Symkyn, was waiting for them as they turned into Paternoster Row. In return for Seb's invitation to join in the feast, the old man had been busy, gathering nature's bounty from the hedgerows to make ivy garlands for the women to wear over their caps or veils and sprigs of holly for the men to sport in their hats.

In the Foxley house, the doors from the parlour and the workshop, on either side of the passage from the front door to the kitchen, had been propped open. Work desks had been moved aside so that the trestles and boards could be set up in line, extending from the parlour, across the passage, into the workshop. Such a board, spread with snowy linen, was worthy of any grand manor, Seb thought, watching proudly as Emily, Rose and Nessie carried platters, dishes and bowls from the kitchen.

'Leave a place for the two large chargers,' Emily told Nessie, as the wench set down a tray of roasted pigeons on the side board in the parlour to await carving. 'Wash your hands everyone and take a seat, if you will.'

They queued at the laver bowl to rinse their hands in warm rosewater, then Tom directed everyone to their place at table, as determined by Mistress Em who'd spent hours deciding not only who should take precedence but who would wish to be close to whom. Old Symkyn posed a problem. He was roughly the age of Dame Ellen – which should give him high status – but as a lowly beggar, he ought to be seated in humble wise, with young Jack. In truth, Emily wished Seb hadn't invited the old man but Christmas meant charity to all, so she'd said naught of it, just thought of it as her Christian duty and smiled as Symkyn crowned her cap with a circlet of ivy. At least he looked as though he'd washed at the conduit and didn't smell too bad in cold weather.

Tom and Nessie were to act as servitors, so they sat in the midst of the board where it crossed the passage, on the side closest to the kitchen so they could easily fetch and carry. Dame Ellen was seated at the head of the table in the parlour, which was warmed by the fire, with her son Dick, his wife Bella Bowen and little Janie. The elderly woman didn't see her granddaughter very often and there would be much to say about the little maid's growth and progress. Seb sat at the far end of the table, in the workshop. Here there were only two brazier baskets so Emily had sat the hardier folk there: her father and brother opposite Jude and Rose. Symkyn and Jack sat opposite Tom and Nessie, their backs to the front door. If there was a draught, those two could best withstand it, she decided. Emily had positioned herself just within the parlour, next to Tom, such that she could make a hasty dash to the kitchen, if needs be.

Seb began the meal with a prayer of thanks for good food and good company then Dick Langton and Jude were tasked with carving the roasted geese at either end of the board. Fine white bread, a stuffing of sage and onion and a sharp gooseberry sauce accompanied the birds. Then pigeons, a leek pottage with savoury dumplings and apple fritters. Finally, to Jack's delight, came a huge Christmas Pie, shaped like a cradle, complete with a Christ Child, moulded from salt-crust pastry and gilded with gold leaf. The babe seemed quite lifelike, betraying Master Seb's artist's handiwork. As promised, when the lid of the pie was lifted off and the steaming contents spooned out, Jack was given the first helping and told to make a wish. It was fortunate, from Jack's point of view, that the Langtons' little maid had fallen asleep, sucking on an apple fritter and there was no one to contest his position as the youngest at table.

'I wish...' he began, taking his spoon to the glorious mixture of chopped meats, spices, dried apricots, currants, dates, suet and sugar but a chorus from the grown-ups reminded him that the wish had to remain a secret. 'Oh, well, I won't tells yer then wot I wished fer, will I?'

Having received his helping, Jude stood up.

'I know I'm not the youngest here by a long way,' he said. 'Even so, I have a wish to make and this one cannot be kept secret.' He took a spoonful of the pie filling, chewed and swallowed. 'My wish is to make Rose my wife, if she will have me?'

A few gasps of surprise were all that broke the silence. Seb's mind was racing: Jude – a confirmed bachelor, if ever there was one, who said marriage was not for him – had known Rose for a matter of weeks, barely a month. All eyes turned to the young woman in question as she sat, looking stunned, wide-eyed and extraordinarily pretty.

'I understand,' Jude said, 'You need time to think upon the matter.' He sat down heavily, perhaps embarrassed that Rose hadn't cried out in great delight and accepted his proposal on the instant.

Rose stood then, also with her spoon full of meats and fruits.

'I need no time, Jude Foxley. I know my answer – knew it the first time I saw you.' She ate her mouthful slowly while everyone, especially Jude, held their breath. 'I wish, wholeheartedly, that you should be my husband.'

Everyone clapped and cheered and wassailed Jude and Rose with cups of spiced ale and mulled Gascon wine. Jude produced a little silken pouch from his purse. It contained a dainty gold ring, set with a stone of lapis lazuli.

'I pray that it fits,' he said. 'If it does, shall we declare ourselves betrothed here and now?'

'Why not? All our friends are present.' Rose held out her hand and Jude slipped the ring on. It fitted perfectly.

'In which case I, Jude Foxley, shall take thee, the beautiful Rose Glover, to be my lawful spouse in the New Year, as soon as be convenient for us both.' He grinned widely and made to kiss her but she put her hand over his mouth to prevent it.

'Wait. You be too eager.' She cleared her throat. 'I, Rose Glover, shall likewise take thee, my beloved Jude Foxley, to be my husband whenever 'tis fitting. This I vow with all my heart. Now. You may kiss me.' She held her cheek towards him but Jude took her head in his hands and turned it towards him, so that he could plant a lusty, smacking kiss on her ruby lips. This time, he had no need of mistletoe.

The afternoon passed in merriment and jollity. Jude played the pipes, Stephen Appleyard had brought his hurdy-gurdy and they all joined in singing and dancing. Admittedly, Seb was far more able to sing than dance – having never learned the latter because of his poorly leg – but Rose brooked no refusal when they came to a dance where, in a change of places, the woman asked the menfolk to dance. Seb found himself cavorting down the passage, through the kitchen and out into the yard beyond, as Rose taught him the steps. He would never be a fine dancer but he found he enjoyed the experience beyond measure. The only sour note of the whole day came when he told Emily that he had to go over to St Mary-le-Bow church, to take Lawrence Ducket some supper. They were in the kitchen where Em was piling yet more platters with cold meats, cheeses and sweetmeats for their guests and he was searching for a basket in which to put food and drink for Lawrence.

'You're not going to St Mary's now, while all our guests are still here,' she told him. 'I cannot prepare the wassail bowl as well as seeing to the food. You said you would do it, Sebastian. I can't do everything at once.'

'But I made a promise to Marjory that I would be certain Lawrence was cared for. I cannot break my word, Em.'

'Then keep your oath, by all means, but send someone else in your stead with the food. I need you here.'

'Mm. I suppose that would do well enough, so long as Lawrence is fed. I'll send Tom.'

'No, Seb. Not Tom. He so rarely sees Bella since she wed Dick Langton, at least let the lad spend time with his sister and little niece. Besides, he's useful at serving. Send that useless urchin and his dog. You know, they nearly upset the whole board at dinner, the pair of them.'

'But they didn't.'

'No, fortunately Rose saved the situation by grabbing that accursed dog by the scruff.'

'Jack didn't do it of a purpose, sweetheart.'

'He never does, does he? Send them over to St Mary's and I can serve supper without fear of being tripped up or trestles overturning. Here. Take this basket and choose your meats for Lawrence – not all the best bits, mind.'

'Thank you, Em.'

Jack did as he was asked. With Little Beggar trotting along at his side and taking time to investigate the nooks and corners of Cheapside, wherever tasty morsels might have been dropped by revellers and not yet stolen away by other creatures of the dark, Jack's only fear was that Master Seb might forget to set aside some supper for him. The sounds of laughter and merrymaking issued from houses and taverns as he skipped by, eager to have his task done and get back to Paternoster Row, where roasted chestnuts and storytelling were promised for after supper. Already, the short hours of winter daylight were dimming but a glorious sunset of crimson and purple was painting the western sky behind him. Master Seb would have admired it so. St Paul's mighty spire pointed heavenwards, black against the painted sky. Jack felt proud of himself: he was beginning to think like his master.

The door of the Green Man tavern stood wide. Jack heard raucous singing – a bawdy song indeed – and paused to listen to the words. Not even knowing the meanings of some, he understood enough to blush hot. He'd try to remember the song, to tell Tom later, to snort and giggle over in their attic beds. A couple of drunken fellows came staggering out the door. One tripped upon the step and dragged his companion down with him. The pair lay laughing in the street until one rolled and threw up his bellyful of ale and the other cursed and pummelled him for soiling his jerkin. Jack side-stepped the mess and headed towards the door of St Mary-le-Bow.

Vespers had just ended, though the congregation had been few, and the priest, Father Thornbury was busy snuffing candles, leaving just one upon the altar to light the darkness.

'Master Ducket is in the vestry,' the priest told Jack when he enquired. 'The brazier is warm in there. I told him he could bide there awhile. I'm off home. Close the door when you leave, lad. I don't want stray dogs and pigs wandering in, befouling God's house. Heaven knows the congregation smells bad enough. I'll be burning extra incense on the morrow to sweeten the place.' The priest came over and lifted the napkin covering Jack's basket. He helped himself to couple of cold savoury dumplings. 'Cannot resist the temptation. Have to do a penance later,' he laughed. Then he left.

Jack found the goldsmith in the vestry, sitting so close to the brazier basket it was a wonder he didn't scorch. He was swathed in furs and blankets yet Jack could hear the man's teeth chattering with cold. It seemed old folk were more prone to the shivers. Jack hardly noticed the chill, even though his breath puffed misty clouds in the vestry air.

'I brunged yer supper, Master Ducket, like Master Seb told me to.'

'I'm grateful, indeed, lad. I'd give you a penny for your trouble except I have no coin.' The goldsmith took the basket and started to eat.

'There was dumplin's but that greedy priest scoffed 'em.'

'No matter. Your master has given me more than enough that I may survive the night. This ham is very good.'

'Aye. Mistress is a fair cook. I like her sweetmeats best.'

'Are there any in here?' Lawrence rummaged in the basket and discovered a comfit dish of dates stuffed with marchpane and honeyed pears. 'Ah, yes. Shall we share them?'

As they chewed and sucked at sticky fingers, the goldsmith told Jack of the games he had played with his brothers in their childhood days. Lawrence was a gifted teller of tales and Jack was enthralled by stories of mischief and mayhem.

'Did yer really set the cat's tail afire, master?'

'Well, in truth, the foolish creature did it itself, leaping onto the board and waving its tail through the candle flame. Such a stink of singed fur. Then it shot out of the window like a bolt loosed from a crossbow. We never saw it again which was a pity, our mother said, as it was a fine mouser.

'Now, youngster, the food is gone and you'd best take your basket and be off home. 'Tis nigh dark and you don't have a torch or lantern. Though, it being Christmas, I can't think that anyone would do you harm. Thank your master for the food. God be with you, lad.'

Jack stuffed the soiled napkin and empty dishes back in the basket anyhow and called to his dog. Beggar, having enjoyed a morsel of pigeon, had been dozing by the brazier, twitching in a doggy dream, but was on his paws, ready to go in an instant.

Out in the nave, it was colder. Jack's shoes and Beggar's claws pattered on the tiled floor. Then Jack heard voices outside, in the church porch. He would have thought naught of it except that Beggar began to growl. And the little dog was never wrong.

'Shh, Beggar.' Jack pulled the mongrel with him into a recess behind the font. 'Shh. Make no sound,' he whispered, clutching Beggar to him and muffling his growls in the folds of his cloak as the door creaked open.

Ten or maybe a dozen men and one woman came in. At first, Jack thought they might have come in out of the cold, the men intending a bit of fun with the woman. That didn't seem right in a church.

'Find the bugger,' one of the men ordered. 'He's here somewhere.'

Jack shrank back as far as he could. He recognised the man. Why were they looking for him? What had he done amiss now such that Sheriff Stocker, no less, was after him? He knew some of the others too, Beadle Draper and Under-sheriff Rigby. He'd had, er, 'dealings' with both in the past.

The woman was wailing now and Jack feared the men were hurting her but she cried out 'I want Lawrence Ducket to pay for his crime! He should be strung up, not skulking here as if he's done naught wrong.'

A half dozen or so rough-looking fellows were searching the church. Jack was terrified that they would find him and Beggar. The dog was squirming to escape from his cloak but Jack held on grimly. Now wasn't the time for Beggar to reveal their hiding place.

'Be still,' Jack mouthed into the fur by the dog's ear and the creature quieted.

It didn't take long before they found their quarry. Lawrence's bellows of protest echoed through the church as they dragged him out of the vestry and into the nave.

'Shut yer noise,' one of the rough fellows shouted and backhanded the goldsmith across the mouth.

'No! None of that, you fool,' said the sheriff. 'I told you: no marks of violence upon the body. Use the sheet. That's what it's for. And bring that ladder.'

'Make the bastard suffer,' the woman insisted, 'For what he did to my poor Ralph.'

'Fear not, Alice, he'll pay the price in full. We'll see that justice is done. He won't escape us by claiming sanctuary.'

Jack couldn't see much in the gloom from his place behind the font but he could hear everything. Master Ducket's protests stopped of a sudden.

'Pull it tighter,' he heard the woman say.

There were sounds of scuffling but they too soon ceased.

'Now string him up.' Sheriff Stocker was striding down the aisle towards the font but he passed by without seeing the hunched figure hiding there.

Men were grunting with the effort. There was a sound like rope creaking, sawing against wood. Jack kept his eyes closed tight but he knew what they were doing. Scalding tears squeezed from betwixt his eyelids, turning cold upon his cheeks but he dared not move to wipe them away. Then the men left, two of them carrying a ladder which clouted the door post, sending a splinter flying.

'Serves you right, Lawrence Ducket. May you rot in hell, you monster.' With those parting words, the woman also went out.

St Mary's fell silent.

Jack crept out of his hiding place. He didn't want to look but his eyes were drawn upward; he couldn't help it.

In the light of the solitary candle, the bulk of Lawrence Ducket hung limp, dangling from a roof beam, suspended by a torn length of bed sheet, swaying slightly.

Beggar, released, scampered out of the church door that had been left ajar. Jack tiptoed after, muffling his sobs until he was sure no one still lurked outside, waiting for him. And then he fled.

The Foxley household was a joyous place that evening. Jude and Rose were in charge of roasting the chestnuts over the fire in the parlour, though with so many kisses and murmuring of sweet-nothings going on, it was a wonder the nuts weren't all charred to blackened ash. Stephen Appleyard was telling the tale of Sir Gawain and the Green Knight, an old seasonal favourite that the carpenter told with relish, giving it a woodworker's twist in that King Arthur's legendary Round Table was most ingeniously constructed and had magical powers of its own.

When Jack returned, flinging his basket into a corner and slumping down on a stool, everyone was too engrossed in the antics of a magic flying table, transporting Gawain across a fantastical world of snow and icy mountains, to notice. Except Seb.

As promised, a platter of delicacies had been set aside for him.

'You must be hungry, Jack,' Seb said, passing him the dish piled with goodies. 'You were gone so long, I was beginning to worry about you. Did Master Ducket detain you? Was the food to his liking?'

Jack made some strange sound, half sob, half groan, shoved the platter aside and ran from the parlour. Moments later, his feet could be heard pounding across the floor overhead as he ran to the ladder that went up to the attic room he shared with Tom.

'How strange,' Seb said, 'I've never known Jack to refuse food afore.'

'There's no mystery, husband,' Em said, having found the basket. 'He's stuffed himself with Lawrence's food, I'll wager. Every scrap is gone and your friend is probably wondering why you forgot him.'

'I'm sure that is untrue, Em. Jack wouldn't do that. He would never disobey me so.'

'That rascal deserves a good beating, if you ask me.'

'No. I'll not beat anyone on Christmas Day. Besides, why do you think he ate what was in the basket?'

'Why else would he not want his supper unless his belly be full already and guilt has overcome his appetite?'

Chapter 3

THE WEATHER remained fine on the morning of the feast of St Stephen. Seb was still wondering at his brother's astounding betrothal. Not that Rose wasn't a wonderful lass and suitable, just that Jude always mocked him for having been wed at all. And what of Jack? The lad seemed unwell, late rising from his bed and leaving his breakfast pottage barely tasted. Perhaps yesterday's abundance of rich food had been too much for the lad. No doubt seeing the Mystery Plays this afternoon would restore his humours.

They were all looking forward to the entertainment – except perhaps Jude who had been given a role in the pageant of the Three Kings. The Stationers' and Goldsmiths' Guilds had combined their talents and props this year and Jude had hoped to be chosen to play one of the leading parts, imagining himself robed royally with a bejewelled diadem about his brow. Instead he was to be Herod's messenger, garbed plainly and with but a single line of speech. He was not impressed.

Seb was out early, hastening to take sustenance to Lawrence, for fear Em was correct in thinking Jack had eaten the goldsmith's supper himself. In which case, Lawrence would be in need. The eastern sky was just showing a rosy glow that set off the black tracery of the naked branches and the few remaining yellowed leaves on the hazel tree by Cordwainer Street turned to gold and sepia. Roofs and fences shimmered with frost, like the crystallised fruits on yesterday's sweetmeats.

As he entered the church, calling out to his friend, the first rays of sunlight burst through the great east window. Such beauty mocked the horror that Seb discovered. His friend's body, hideous against the light, rocked in the draught from the door. Seb closed his eyes. Surely they were seeing something that was not truly there at all. But a second look confirmed the same.

'Oh, dear God. Lawrence.' Seb made the sign of the cross repeatedly. 'What has befallen you? May God have mercy.'

Seb summoned the priest from his breakfast in the house next door. The man was dismayed and rightly so but seemed more upset that his church had been desecrated than over the horrible death of one of his parishioners.

'Suicide!' Father Thornbury shrieked. 'God rot his blasphemous soul. How dare he taint this holy place with so heinous a crime against the Almighty? How dare he count himself a Christian and then stoop to such a devilish action?'

'Will you at least give him the benefit of the last rites?' Seb said, interrupting the priest's outrage.

'I most certainly will not. Suicides deserve nothing of the kind.'

'I will pay,' Seb offered.

'His stinking corpse will be flung in a ditch and left for the crows and rats to feast on. Such is the punishment for taking one's own life.'

'But, please...'

'Plead all you want. Holy Church washes its hands of his kind. There is naught more to be said upon the matter. I'll send for Master Bulman. Let the deputy-coroner determine cause of death, officially, as if it isn't obvious enough.' The priest stormed out.

Seb knelt at the chancel steps. If the priest would do nothing to aid Lawrence's soul, Seb could at least offer up a layman's prayers and light a candle for him. What a great weight of sorrow and remorse Lawrence must have suffered beneath, such that it drove him to this extremity. Poor man. And how distraught Marjory would be... Sweet heaven. He was going to have to break the news to her. He was about to light a taper when Father Thornbury returned. He strode over and knocked the candle from Seb's hand.

'No candles for such sacrilege. I won't have it, not for one who commits the crime of Judas.'

'I-I was lighting it for his wife, Marjory.' That was not entirely true but Seb didn't care for the priest's attitude. 'She is innocent of any wrong-doing but is going to be broken hearted at what has come to pass.'

'Oh. Very well. Do as you must. I have the coroner coming – to no point whatever since the means of death is blatantly obvious – and men to get that thing, that obscenity out of my church. If you want, you can assist them. It isn't going to be easy. 'Tis a wonder he managed it.'

Indeed, Seb thought, it most certainly was a wonder. How had Lawrence climbed onto the roof beam? It was too far away from the rood loft to reach the beam from there. Almost any other beam would have been easier but Lawrence had chosen the one in the very centre of the nave. And no sign of a ladder. Possibly a rope could have been thrown over the beam and tied off but Lawrence hung from a short length of bed sheet. There seemed no other way but for him to have climbed up there, but how? Unless he had someone aid him? Or force him?

Seb shivered. The more he considered it, the more he became convinced that his friend's death was no suicide. It was murder. But how to prove it?

Deputy-Coroner Bulman arrived, looked up at the hanged man, nodded and shrugged. He did naught to assist the fellows who came to take down Lawrence's sorry corpse but watched, arms folded, tapping his foot impatiently. Once it was done, the coroner peered down at the body, scratching at his ruddy jowls in contemplation and nodding some more before leaving the church, his unsavoury task accomplished. The official paperwork could wait until a later date. In the church doorway, the deputy-coroner met Sheriff Stocker who had also come to view the scene. There was a moment of palpable tension as the sheriff had to step aside for the deputy-coroner who, being appointed by the king, took precedence over a man appointed to office by the Lord Mayor. In the end, the coroner's over-ample weight of flesh was enough to win the wordless contest. The pair did not even exchange a greeting but their scowls said more than words could convey.

All the while, Seb was praying silently because Father Thornbury refused to permit him to do so openly. That his friend, so full of life, his humours but recently a mix of merriment and disputation, could come to this in so short a space, reduced to an inert bag of bones. And what of his soul? Was that now condemned to torment everlasting? The wretched priest was insisting upon it.

'What now, sir priest?' one of the men asked when Lawrence lay upon the floor of the nave. 'What do we do with it?'

Seb flinched. His friend was not an 'it' but a man.

'I told you. Take it to the crossroads, where Cock Lane and Holbourne Hill meet Seacole and Cow Lanes. We don't want an unquiet spirit finding its way back here to trouble us anew.

I have problems enough since the coroner has ruled 'suicide'. My church has been violated and the bishop will order it to be closed up until he deems it fitting to reconsecrate it. Who knows when that may be?'

'You want us t' bury it, sir?'

'Most certainly not. Throw it in the ditch. The kites and rats can deal with it.'

'No! I beg you,' Seb said, taking hold of the priest's vestment.

'Unhand me!'

'Forgive me, sir, but please allow my friend's body to be buried at least. He deserves...'

'He deserves nothing. A suicide forgoes all Christian burial rites. You know that. There can be no exception made for personal sentiment. I advise you to forget him. Any attempt on your part to mitigate the lack of a proper funeral can only serve to taint your own soul. You have been warned.'

Despite the warning, Seb followed the men with their handcart, along Cheapside and the Shambles, passed the Grey Friars and out of Newgate. Beyond the church of St Sepulchre and the Saracen's Head tavern, they turned right on Seacole Lane. A little farther along, where Holbourne Hill came down from the west, the Fleet River ran sluggishly in its deep ditch, fetid and noisome. Here the men stripped the corpse of its fine fur-lined gown before upending the cart, tipping its load into the ditch. Then, without a backward glance, they turned and trundled the handcart back towards Newgate, leaving Seb standing alone.

Once the men were out of sight, he climbed down into the mire, to arrange the body in a seemly fashion, straightening the remaining clothing. He tried to cross his friend's hands upon his breast but the rigors of death made it impossible. With his own clothes now infested with the stench of the Fleet, his boots caked in stinking black mud, Seb struggled back up onto Seacole Lane.

Tears ran down his face as he recited, from memory, the Office of the Dead, as much as he could recall. The priest's warning meant naught to him since he was sure Lawrence had been murdered and was innocent of the crime of Judas. Then he too returned within the city gate. At least he could tell Marjory he had done what he could for husband's soul, small comfort though that would be.

'Where have you been, Sebastian Foxley? There's work to done afore we attend the Mystery Plays this afternoon, or have you forgotten we still need to earn a living? And look at you! You stink! What in the name of all that's holy have you been doing? 'Tis hours – a whole morning gone – since you set out to take Lawrence Ducket his breakfast...'

'Hold off, Em, for pity's sake.' Seb held up his hands in a gesture of surrender before removing his mantle and hanging it from its peg by the door.

'Dear Lord, Seb.' Emily inspected the garment and sniffed at it, screwing up her face in distaste. 'Did you use this to swab out a pig sty? It reeks. How am I supposed to clean it afore you wear it this afternoon, eh?'

'Does it matter?' he asked, sinking onto the nearest stool by the kitchen fire, belatedly realising the water in the ditch had soaked his breeches and chilled him to the core.

'Of course it matters. What sort of half-decent goodwife would have her husband seen in public stinking worse than a midden? Oh, no. Your boots! Get them off. See what they've done to my clean floor. You are so thoughtless.'

'Lawrence Ducket is dead and I have just come from informing his widow. Marjory is distraught. I knew not what to do for her. I was useless in the face of so much weeping.'

'I was on my hands and knees scrubbing the flagstones for an hour or more while you were out and now look. I need not have taken the trouble. What a waste of my time.'

'Lawrence Ducket is dead,' Seb repeated.

'What? How can that be? You took him food this morn.'

'I found him dead, Em. He was hanged from a roof beam in the church.' Seb clamped his hands over his mouth but could hold back the sobs no longer. He broke down and wept for his friend. 'They say he was a suicide but 'tis not true. He was killed. I know.'

Laughter could be heard in the passage as Jude and Rose came from the workshop. Jude had being showing his betrothed how to collate the separate gatherings of a text – amid much petting and giggling – but had achieved a surprising amount of work which now required some refreshment.

'Who's been killed?' Jude asked, having overheard his brother's last few words.

'Lawrence Ducket, apparently,' Em said, handing Seb a table napkin to staunch his tears.

'Oh, Seb, how terrible,' Rose said, putting her arm around him. 'Is there anything I can do? What of his poor wife? Such a kindly woman...we should aid her, if we may? What's to be done?'

Gradually, with young Tom come to join them from the workshop, over cups of ale all round, Seb told them of the morning's sad happenings. Em bustled about, attempting to do three tasks at once: freshening her goodman's foul-smelling clothes, trying to clean his boots and prepare dinner, all the while adding her own comments to the unfolding tale and the discussion that followed it. In the end, she gave the boots to Nessie to clean, out in the yard. Rose took over the stirring of the pottage pot and the dicing of bacon and yesterday's leftover meats, while Em set about Seb's mantle with rosewater, a sponge and a stout clothes brush, muttering about the stink and the state of the heavy woollen garment.

'Well, if the coroner agreed it was suicide, why do you think otherwise?' Em asked Seb.

'I just don't see any way in which he could have done it. He would have required a ladder to reach that beam.'

'Does the church have a ladder?'

'Even if it does, Em, there was no ladder there in the nave. If Lawrence did use one to climb up, where did it go? Someone else must have taken it away. In which case, either Lawrence had help or... Or I fear he was hanged by a third party – or parties, more like. He was a big man to be lifted so high or forced to climb up.'

They all sat down to a belated dinner. Seb chewed with little idea of what he was eating. But there was a space upon one bench.

'Where is Jack?' Seb asked. 'I've never known him miss a meal afore. Thinking upon it, I barely saw him this morn at all.'

'After you left, he returned to his bed, sulking, the idle little shirker,' Em said. 'He's a work-shy layabout in need of a hefty thrashing, as I told you yesterday.'

'He must be sick, Em. You know Jack, never still for two moments together. He wouldn't lie abed unless he be ill. I'll go up to him. See what ails the lad.'

'Finish your food first. You think I haven't made certain of that already? He has no fever, no rash and no pain. He tells me there's naught wrong. He just hides beneath the bed sheets, clutching that damned dog to himself, like a drowning man to a floating timber. By all means speak to him and take a birch rod with you. Tell him I'll not waste a crumb of food on one who refuses to work for it.'

With dinner eaten and the table cleared, the dishes and pots washed, everyone was ready to walk along to Cheapside, to watch the pageant wagons roll past, according to the St Stephen's day tradition. Rose was particularly keen to see Jude play his part in the story of the Three Kings, even if it was but a small role. Yet would the pageant happen after all? Lawrence Ducket had been chosen to play Herod – as he had the year before, to great acclaim – but without him, the pageant might have to be abandoned. But there would be other guilds to tell other stories from the Bible, all well worth braving the cold to watch.

Only Seb stayed home, much concerned for Jack and hardly of a humour to be entertained.

'Jack? I've brought you some ale,' Seb said, managing to climb the ladder to the loft one-handed – a feat not so easy with his hip stiff and aching from the dip in icy water earlier. 'You must be thirsty, lad, having missed dinner.'

Jack was invisible, burrowed beneath the blankets. Seb turned them aside; found a tousled head of dark hair and the pale fur of a dog's ear.

'Come, Jack, what be amiss with you, lad? You can't hide abed forever.'

'I can't come out, can I? They'll kill us if they find us.' Jack's voice was so muffled by the covers, Seb thought he must have misheard.

'What foolishness is this? No one is going to hurt you. When have I ever beaten you? Never, as you well know. Whatever you have done Jack, I promise you...'

'I ain't done nuffin, 'onest, but I fink them buggers seed me an' I know they'll kill me an' Beggar, if they find us.'

'You are perfectly safe, lad. Now, come, drink your ale at least.'

'I ain't safe, I'm tellin' yer, master.' Jack sniffed up snot and pulled the pillow over his head. 'I ain't.'

Seb lifted the pillow away.

'If you truly think someone intends you harm, then we must inform Sheriff Stocker...'

'Nah!' Jack screeched, 'Yer can't. Yer mustn't. Please, master. Not 'im.' The lad grabbed Seb's jerkin and clung on. 'Don't tell a soul, will yer, please Master Seb? Me an' Beggar don't wanna die, do we, Beg?'

'Easy, easy, lad. No one is going to hurt you.' Seb held Jack close, rocking gently. 'You and Beggar are quite safe. Hush. There is naught to be feared. Breathe calm and slowly now. That's it. All is well. Be easy in your mind.' Seb continued to murmur soft words and rock until he felt the tension easing in the lad's body. Eventually, sleep claimed the youngster and Seb lay him down, tucking the blankets close. However, the dog had other needs and made it plain that he wanted to go down the ladder. Seb carried the dog down and then let the creature find his own way to the yard below.

Jack stirred.

'Beggar? Where's Beggar?' he cried.

'Don't be alarmed. He had to go to the yard to piss. He'll be back.'

'Not if they see 'im. They'll know where I am, Gawd save us! Wot can I do, master? They're gonna kill me fer sure.'

'Now Jack, I've told you. Believe me when I tell you that you are quite safe. And Beggar too. Listen? You hear his paws on the landing? I'll fetch him up.' Seb made for the ladder again.

'Make sure no bugger sees yer, master.'

'In our own home? Whoever do you think will harm us? You fret needlessly, lad.'

'But I seed 'em do it an' if they know...'

'You saw who do what?'

'Them. Them wot killed Master Ducket. Me an' Beggar seed everyfink, didn't we? But I daren't say nuffink cos if them buggers finded out...'

Seb forgot about the dog and returned to sit on the edge of Jack's bed.

'Who did you see, Jack? Now think carefully and tell me true, everything you can remember. Do not fear. No one is going to be angry with you, I promise.'

'But you'll tell them, I knows yer will.'

'Why would I tell the evil-doers?'

'Cos yer will. Cos yer say we 'ave t' tell the sheriff or the beadle or somebody.'

'Well, aye, we should.'

'Then I can't say nuffink, can I? Jus' go away an' leave us be, can't yer!' Jack buried his head beneath the pillow once more.

Seb sighed, too weary to try any longer. He would leave Jack to sort out matters in his own mind for a while but first, he lifted Beggar back up the ladder. At least the little animal seemed to give the lad some small measure of comfort.

The others returned from watching the mystery plays.

'You missed a truly worthy performance, little brother,' Jude told Seb. He seemed to have grown by inches and his chest broadened. 'You'll ne'er guess who was asked to replace Lawrence Ducket as Herod?' Jude strutted around the kitchen like a victorious fighting cock.

'I don't doubt you'll tell me.' Seb was not overly interested. He was still attempting to fathom Jack's inordinate fear of men in authority. Of course, as a street urchin, the lad had suffered close encounters with various officers of the law at one time or other. Had one of them beaten him too harshly or been cruel to the lad? Seb wondered if that was the simple explanation although the matter seemed to run deeper than that.

'Me! You ought to have seen me, Seb. I was brilliant, terrifying. I had the audience quaking when I ordered the slaying of the Innocents. Mothers shielded their little ones and babes bawled. I had such majestic presence.'

'Oh.'

'Oh? Is that all you can think to say? Tell him, Rose. Tell him what you thought of my performance.'

'It was, er, memorable,' Rose said, choosing her word with care.

'Aye, especially when the crown slipped down over his eyes and he couldn't see and tripped over King Balthazar's foot,' Tom added, smirking.

'Was that my fault? The crown was made to fit Lawrence. His head was bigger than mine.'

'I very much doubt that,' Emily said. Tom and Nessie joined with her in laughter. Only Rose tried to soothe Jude.

'You looked so fine in the purple velvet robes I could imagine you as King Edward himself.'

'But he's fat as an ale barrel these days,' Jude protested. 'Are you saying I've got a paunch like his?'

'No, of course you haven't. I meant that you could pass for royalty dressed so grandly and every inch a prince.'

'Aye, well, just so long as that be all you meant.'

'Come. All of you. Out of my kitchen, if you want supper on time.' Emily shooed the menfolk from her realm so that she, Rose and Nessie could prepare a meal. 'Unless you would aid us in peeling onions and boning mackerel?'

Seb, Jude and Tom preferred to retire to the parlour but Emily called out:

'And what of Jack? Am I cooking for that idle jackanapes or not? Where is he? Not still abed, surely?'

'I fear so,' Seb said.

'Not for much longer he isn't.' With that, Emily fetched her broom. 'I'll have him out of that bed before you can say "St Stephen". I warned him, so I did.'

'No, Em. The lad be in a state of terror as it is. I promised him that none would do him any hurt.'

'He's a lazy little toad and I'll not abide such behaviour, Seb.'

'Please, Em. Show forbearance in this case. I believe Jack saw who killed Lawrence Ducket.'

52

'Killed him? No one killed him. That's just your fancy because he was your friend. He died by his own hand. 'Tis the talk of Cheapside.'

'That is not so. It was murder and Jack knows who did it but he will not tell me their names.'

'Which proves he is lying, making up stories to excuse his idleness.'

'He fears that if he reveals their names, they will come and kill him too. The poor lad is terrified, Em.'

'Such nonsense. I never heard the like. And you believe him?'

'I do.'

'Then you be a fool indeed, Sebastian Foxley.'

Before supper, Seb returned to the loft, hoping to tempt Jack down to the kitchen to eat. The lad must be famished by now. The dog also. Maybe, if Beggar came to eat, Jack could be persuaded to join them at the board.

'Jack? There is mackerel for supper and apple dumplings – your favourite dish. I'm sure Beggar would enjoy...'

'No! I'm not comin' down, not never, master. Beggar can, if he wants, but I can't, can I? Yer knows that. Or else I'm a dead 'un.'

'See sense, lad. I know you fear those evil-doers but you cannot starve yourself, or you will have achieved their aim in any case.'

'Yer could bring us food up here, couldn't yer?'

'No, Jack. Mistress Em will never allow it unless you be very sick. And I am no servant to wait upon you like some puffed-up lordling. Come down to supper and hear of Master Jude's efforts to play the role of Herod. It will make you laugh for certain.'

'It won't. Herod killed innocent little 'uns, jus' like them buggers'll kill me, if they sees me.'

'If you tell me their names, at least I'll know for whom we should keep a watch.' With a sigh, Seb eased himself down to sit upon the bedside. He felt tired and his still-mending ribs were aching. 'Come, tell me.'

'Yer won't never b'lieve us, if I telled yer.'

'I may but you'll not know unless you confide in me.' Seb stroked the lad's tear-streaked cheek.

'I ain't canfidin' in nuffin!' Jack sobbed. 'Yer'll never b'lieve I seed Sheriff Stocker an' the beadle an' the under-sheriff stringin' up Master Ducket, will yer?'

Seb was too shocked for speech.

'See. I knowed yer wouldn't cos yer fink them buggers is the law. But they ain't. They killed 'im. Now yer knows why I can't never stop hidin' away in me bed an' yer mustn't tell nobody.'

'Oh, Jack. No wonder you be so afeared.'

'You do b'lieve me then?'

'I think you best tell me everything that you saw come to pass in St Mary's. Everything, Jack.'

'You don't fink I'm lyin', do yer?'

'No.'

'Well, your supper has gone cold – again. Why do I waste my time, toiling over pots and platters for a husband who doesn't eat my food?'

'Forgive me, Em. I had to listen to Jack's tale. 'Tis disquieting indeed. I be unsure what to do about it.'

'It could have waited until after supper.'

'No. The lad was at last ready to tell it. I could not make him delay for fear he would change his mind. Nessie, take some supper up to the lad, please.'

'Oh, no. I'm not having him taken food when he can't be bothered to come down to the kitchen to eat. I forbid it.'

'Emily. Just this one time you will allow it. Now do as I say, Nessie.'

'Aye, master.' The wench even made Seb a half-hearted courtesy, seeing the stern look in his steel-grey eyes, before preparing a tray to take up to the loft.

Emily was staring at her goodman. Seb never asserted himself so. She was outraged at her orders being gainsaid but, for once, she kept silent.

If only Jude or even Gabriel still lived here, Seb thought, they could have discussed what ought to be done, advised him, at least. But Em was in no humour to pay heed and Rose, though a sympathetic listener, was a young lass. What would she know of the laws of London? Tom might at least provide a male ear but an apprentice should not have to bear such responsibility. He had to share the burden of this knowledge with someone but they must be sworn to secrecy for the present, before he dared relate Jack's story. Who could he trust?

'I'm going out,' Seb announced, abandoning his supper.

'At this late hour? What cannot wait until tomorrow?' Emily demanded, still vexed.

'I have to speak with Jude.'

'I thought my life would improve when he moved back to Cheapside, yet I swear you still spend more time with that wretch than you do with me. Can you not speak with him when he comes to work in the morn?'

'This is too important to wait, Em.'

She rolled her eyes.

'Of course. Isn't it always so?'

Seb put on his mantle and lit a torch from the fire to light his way, as the law required of a respectable citizen. Only felons went about their unwholesome business in darkness.

'And don't be so hard on poor Jack, either.'

'Poor Jack? What of poor Emily? Do you care one jot for her?'

'You know I do.' He kissed her brow but she pushed him away. Aye, and poor Seb, he thought. I'll be sleeping on the parlour floor again this night, no doubt, sore ribs or not.

Seb stumbled along Cheapside, bone-weary, to the lodging house he and Jude used to share, next door to Dame Ellen Langton, their landlady. Jude had lately moved back, having suffered enough of Emily's sharp tongue at Paternoster Row. Seb prayed that Jude would be there, not carousing in a tavern somewhere, so he was much relieved that Jude opened the door when he knocked.

'A bit late to be visiting, isn't it? Come in, share some ale. It'll be like old times, before you were wed, eh, little brother?'

'Aye, and like those days, I may ask to share your bedchamber.'

'Oh, now I understand. The firebrand has thrown you out, has she?'

'Maybe. Who knows? I have weightier matters to concern me, Jude, and would ask your advice. 'Tis about something to which young Jack bore witness. A grave misdeed and I know not what to do about it.'

'Sebastian Foxley: London's most righteous and up-standing citizen, in a quandary? How can that be? Inform the sheriff of this "misdeed". Surely that's always your way, if not mine?'

'Do not make a jest of it, I beg you.'

Over the ale jug, into the small hours, Seb related Jack's story, in full. Jude cursed and swore, as was his way, but otherwise did not interrupt.

'Bugger it, Seb,' he said when the tale was done and the fire in the hearth burned down to a solitary red eye and little warmth. 'I always knew I was right not to trust the law. Now we have proof.'

'Well, perhaps we do. But who will believe the word of a little lad? I hardly believe it myself except that I cannot explain the absence of a ladder and how else might Lawrence have climbed up?'

The bell of St Martin's-le-Grand nearby tolled the hour of matins, summoning the monks to the first office of the day. It was after midnight.

'Whatever is to be done, it can't be done at this time of night. I think we ought to sleep on it. Are you staying? I'll find you a blanket.'

Chapter 4

Next morn at Paternoster Row

'COME DOWN, Jack. There be naught to fear, lad.' Seb leaned through the trapdoor so his head was up in the loft where the apprentices slept. 'You cannot expect Coroner Bulman to climb up to you.'

'I ain't comin' down, master,' Jack whined, 'Yer knows why not.'

Seb sighed, climbed the remaining rungs of the ladder and stepped into the loft.

'Jack,' he whispered, moving close to the heap of bedding that was the lad's hideaway. 'Have pity, won't you? You must realise the coroner be far too fat to squeeze through that hole. Would you have him wedged there until he wastes away sufficient to get out again?'

Muffled giggles sounded beneath the blanket, just as Seb had hoped.

'How does I know he won't arrest us?'

'Why would he? You have done no wrong. Once you have spoken with Master Bulman, Mistress Em has prepared your favourite breakfast.'

Slowly, reluctantly, a tousled head appeared out of the nest of bedding.

'Yer sure the c'roner ain't one of 'em?'

'You should know better than I, lad: you saw what came to pass in St Mary's, as I did not. Besides, Master Jude knows Coroner Bulman well, serving as his sometime clerk, and he says we can trust him. And you know Master Jude be as suspicious of the law as any man.'

Seb pealed back the last blanket. Perhaps he shouldn't have been surprised but he certainly raised an eyebrow for Jack was fully clothed, right down to his muddy boots and rumpled cloak, in fear of having to flee for his life at a moment's notice. Emily would not be pleased at the filth upon the linen sheets but Seb made no remark, having finally persuaded the lad to leave his bed. Instead, he pulled the youngster's clothing into some semblance of order, smoothed down his unkempt hair that stood on end and smiled – reassuringly, he hoped.

Jack dithered by the ladder.

'You go down first, master, pleeease.'

'You'll not get back in your bed if I do?'

'Nah.'

'Promise upon your oath?'

The lad nodded and crossed himself.

'Promise.'

Seb went down the ladder. Master Bulman waited with Jude on the outside landing.

'He is coming.'

'I don't know what all this fuss is about, Foxley?' Bulman said. 'You say 'tis a most serious matter but the fellow can't be bothered to get out of bed to speak of it.'

'The kitchen will be a warmer place for the interview, sir,' Seb offered. 'My wife will serve mulled ale.'

'Oh, very well. But this had better be worth my time and trouble.'

As Seb and Jude escorted the coroner to the kitchen, Jude whispered to his brother:

'You're certain the little bugger won't make a run for it?'

'He promised me.'

'And you believe the word of that scallywag?'

'Jude, if we don't believe his word that he will come down, then how can we believe the rest of his tale? Are we wasting the coroner's time?'

Finally, when the coroner was already well into his second cup of ale, Jack appeared. Bulman ignored the scruffy lad, thinking he was a menial, a scullery-boy or some such.

'Coroner Bulman,' Seb said, 'This is Jack Tabor. The lad we spoke of.'

'What! A snot-nosed boy? And you would account him a reliable witness? No. No, Master Foxley. I thank you for the ale but my time is too precious to waste...'

'Master Bulman,' Jude said, leaning closer to the coroner like a conspirator. 'I know you have very little liking for Sheriff Stocker. How would it please you to see him removed from office, eh?' Jude had pens, paper and ink ready on the kitchen board to exercise his role as coroner's clerk.

'I should enjoy that indeed, but upon the word of a little toad such as this...'

Seb made a grab for Jack's arm as the lad turned to run from the kitchen.

'See! I told yer, 'e wouldn't b'lieve us, didn't I?' he sobbed, pulling away.

'Make your obeisance, Jack,' Seb told him, 'Properly.' He held the lad by the shoulders, pressing him to make a bow to the coroner. 'Now. Be you ready to tell your story? More ale, Master Bulman, sir?'

The coroner allowed his cup to be replenished, folded his arms and sighed.

'Very well. Do you, Jack...what's his name?'

'Jack Tabor, sir,' Seb said.

'Mm. Well, where is my copy of the Gospels?'

Jude put a much-worn little book into Bulman's hand. As the coroner's clerk upon occasion, he knew to have it ready.

'Put your hand upon the book...no, on second thoughts, wash your hands first, boy.' Jack went to the laver bowl, rinsed his fingers and wiped them on his breeches. 'Now, let's get this done. Do you, Jack Tabor, swear upon holy writ to tell the truth, the whole of the truth and naught else but the truth, so help you Almighty God?'

Jack nodded.

'Speak up!'

'Aye, sir,' Jack squeaked.

Seb patted the lad's arm.

'Don't be afeared,' he said. 'We are all your friends here and you are quite safe.'

Bulman glared at Seb for interrupting.

'Tell me what you think you saw, boy.'

'I don't fink; I knows wot I seed, sir. A gang of 'em came into St Mary's church and strung up poor Master Ducket. He kicked an' shouted but there wos too many of 'em...an' a woman an' all, tellin' 'em t' get on wiv it.'

'A woman?'

'Aye. One fella called 'er Alice. The under-sheriff, I fink it wos. Aye, it were 'im, Thomas Rigby. I knows 'im cos he caught us once...'

'Alice? Did he say her other name?'

'Don't fink so, else I'd remember it, wouldn't I?'

'Indeed. And who else was there?' Bulman sipped his ale. 'You writing all this down, Foxley?'

'Of course,' Jude said, 'Every word.' He finished writing at the bottom of a page and took a fresh sheet of paper, dipping his pen in the ink.

'There wos Sheriff Stocker an' Beadle Draper an' some uvver fellas, rough sorts. I don't fink I ever knowed their names but I seed some of 'em before, ain't I.'

'Would you recognise them, if you saw them again?'

'I'd know the woman, sir, fer certain. An' two o' them ruffians looked ezackerly the same, didn't they, like twins, they wos, wiv reddish hair an' beards.'

'Mm. Sounds like the Rufus twins,' Bulman muttered. 'Note that down, Foxley.'

Jude exchanged a raised-eyebrow look with Seb, having already written the information down.

'An' a bald fella wiv a funny 'and, fingers missing, sort of.'

'Alice At-Bowe's brother, Maurice, has a mangled hand as a remembrance of his days as a soldier,' Jude said, scribbling. 'And he keeps company with the Rufus twins and a pack of bloody scoundrels from his fighting days. It could be them.'

'When I want your opinion, Foxley, I'll ask for it. Now, boy, relate to me the lineaments and apparel of the woman.'

'Wot?'

'Tell Master Bulman what the woman looked like. What was she wearing?' Seb translated.

'Oh, aye. She were tallish fer a woman, wiv big, er, yer know wot I mean.' Jack used his hands to outline imaginary feminine curves. 'Yer know, tits. An' she wos wearin' a fancy veil wot stuck out like linen dryin' on a hedge. Looked daft t' me. An' a green cloak wiv fur – jus' like the colour wot yer painted the Magdalene's gown in that book the uvver day, Master Seb.'

'Terra verde, that was, Jack. Well remembered.'

'Indeed. I don't think we need go into such detail. Now, boy, describe precisely what you saw these folk do to Master Ducket in the church.'

'Yer b'lieve us, then?' Jack asked, hardly daring to think the coroner accepted that he was telling the truth. Refreshed with a cup of ale that Master Seb gave him, the lad told his story once more. There were disquieting details concerning the goldsmith's murder that Jack hadn't mentioned before to his master. No wonder the lad had been in fear for his life.

At last it was done.

'Come, Foxley, bring those papers. We must take this to the Lord Mayor himself. Get warrants for the arrests of all these miscreants. One in particular shall give me the greatest of pleasure. As for you, young Jack Tabor, you may well be asked to attend upon Lord Mayor Josselyn, so get yourself cleaned up and presentable.'

'Me, sir?'

The deputy-coroner departed, taking Jude with him.

Seb set a platter of oatcakes and a bowl of steaming pottage on the board before Jack.

'This ain't me fav'rite, like wot yer said Mistress Em had cooked fer us, is it?' Jack looked accusingly at his master.

'Forgive me, Jack. I realise I set you a poor example but I had to persuade you from your bed somehow, did I not?'

'S'pose, so,' Jack admitted, stuffing an oatcake into his mouth, whole.

Guildhall, London. The Lord Mayor's Court

That afternoon, washed, combed and wearing his Sunday best, Jack was summoned to the Guildhall. It was as well that Master Seb was with him or he might never have had the courage to stand there in the Lord Mayor's court.

Word of such goings-on had spread through the city faster than fire with the wind behind it. The court was crowded indeed.

The accused were escorted in by the sergeants-at-arms in their city livery and lined up before the Lord Mayor, resplendent in his robes, seated high upon the judgement bench. Alice At-Bowe looked bedraggled and frightened. Her fellows in crime were also rumpled and grubby but, by turns, belligerent, scornful and defiant. Only Beadle Draper looked nervous.

Marjory Ducket, by contrast, handsome in her widow's weeds, stood before the assembly. She appeared commendably composed, Seb thought. At the Lord Mayor's invitation, she stood up, facing the crowd of her fellow citizens.

'I bring before this court my case for the murder of my husband, Lawrence Ducket of Cordwainer Street,' she said in a clear voice.

Murder? The word rippled through the court. Had Lawrence Ducket not killed himself, then? After all, a woman could only bring a prosecution to court in the case of her husband being unlawfully killed. Had the rumours been wrong?

'I accuse Alice At-Bowe, Sheriff John Stocker, Beadle Paul Draper, Under-sheriff Thomas Rigby, Maurice At-Bowe, William and Walter Rufus and others of murdering my husband even as he was under the protection of Holy Sanctuary. This is my case.' Marjory returned to her stool beside Seb and sat down, looking small and vulnerable of a sudden.

'You did well, mistress,' Seb said, resting his hand on hers for the briefest of moments to reassure her. Her skin was icy cold beneath his fingertips and he could feel her trembling – or shivering. 'You named Alice At-Bowe first among them. Do you know her personally?' he whispered.

'Know her? The wretched woman had been carrying on with my Lawrence for nigh unto a year, thinking I would not discover their dirty little secret. Then she jilted him, by letter – which I read – telling him she had found a better man. As if that were possible.'

Seb tried to smother his gasp. Lawrence and Alice At-Bowe? Well, that was quite a revelation.

'She led him astray,' Marjory was saying, 'Though he always came back to me, of course. Then she tells him she no longer wants him. Poor Lawrence was quite put out, so distressed, my lamb was. Turning him down for that weedy Ralph Aldgate who's only half the man my Lawrence was. Is it any wonder my goodman came to blows with him? But I shall be revenged upon her. Poor Lawrence.' The widow wiped her eye on her spotless apron.

But the afternoon's surprises were not done yet.

'Go on, Jack, I know your heart be stout enough and brave.' Seb smiled at the lad who stood beside him, rigid with fear, awaiting the summons to give his testimony. 'Just tell the truth. That be all that is asked of you.'

'Wot if they don't fink I am tellin' the troof? Wot then, master?'

'At least we will have done our duty by Master Ducket.'

'But them buggers might still come after me then, mightn't they?'

'I will keep you safe, Jack, never fear.' Seb spoke with a confidence he did not feel. What could he do to protect the lad from such men of rank and authority? If they went free, they would no doubt seek to be avenged on the child who, if naught else, was about to call their reputations into question in front of their fellow citizens. How could a humble artist stand betwixt a lad and the weight of the law? The honest answer was that he could not. He must devise a means of smuggling Jack out of London. Perhaps on a ship bound for the Low Countries, just as they had sent Gabriel Widowson to safety a month since?

In a quivering voice, Jack Tabor made his oath upon the Gospels.

'Speak up, child,' the mayor said, not unkindly. 'My ears are not as young as yours and I would hear every word.'

Jack nodded and when he spoke again his voice was steadier and rang clear through the great hall. No one present that afternoon, especially the jury of twelve good citizens, would miss a single word of the lad's testimony. His concise telling and use of innocent simple words meant that the court seemed to accept the truth of his story. When he had finished, the mayor asked him whether he was utterly certain as to the identity of those he had seen that eve in St Mary's, the lad turned to Seb.

'Wot's idertatty mean, master?'

'Do you recognise and know them by name, Jack?' Seb said.

'Aye, I does.' The lad named the sheriff, the under-sheriff and the beadle, pointing them out to the court. Stocker glared back. Ripley sighed and shook his head. Draper looked as though he was attempting to hide behind the other two.

'How do you know these men by name?' the mayor asked.

'I-I got catched by 'em, didn't I? Lots of times when I w-wos fievin'. But I don't do that no more now I work fer Master Seb, do I?'

Folk laughed in the court but Seb groaned aloud.

'Are you quite well, Sebastian?' Marjory asked.

'They won't believe his story now, will they? The testimony of an admitted thief. Oh, Marjory, I'm so sorry. This has all been to no avail.'

'Don't be so sure. I know most of the jurors and at least half of them have dined at our house at one time or another. Lawrence would account them as friends, I know. They will want to see him avenged.'

Finally, the mayor told Jack he was excused. The lad stepped down and ran to Seb.

'Did I do it right, master? I telled the troof like wot yer said.'

'Aye, so you did, Jack. It was well done.'

'They will find them buggers guilty, won't they?'

'If they do not, the fault will certainly not lay with you, lad. We must wait upon the verdict now.'

The proceedings dragged on. Jack fell asleep, resting against Seb, snoring softly. Marjory sighed at every pronouncement, wringing her hands in her apron until it looked no more pristine than a floor rag. Finally, the case was done and the mayor bade the jury consider their verdict.

Seb could feel his heart pounding, his belly churning like a waterwheel. But the twelve men were merciful and did not prolong his anxiety. One among them stood up.

'You have reached your verdict?' the mayor asked.

'We have, my lord.'

'The defendants will stand and face the court. Now, how do you find the accused Alice At-Bowe?'

'We find her guilty as charged.'

The court gasped. Alice At-Bowe burst into noisy tears. The mayor ignored her.

'How do you find the accused John Stocker?'

'We find him guilty as charged.'

Seb too felt tears threatening – tears of relief – and a lump in his throat that was nigh choking him. He could hardly draw breath.

As Thomas Ripley, Paul Draper and the others were all found guilty Seb realised that Marjory was holding his arm so tightly, her nails dug through his sleeve more deeply with every verdict given. Jack was unable to keep still a moment longer, fidgeting like one suffering a seizure.

'Will they hang 'em, master? They will, won't they, else I shan't be safe ever, shall I?'

'Shh. Just listen, lad.'

After the verdicts were given, sentencing followed. Alice At-Bowe was sentenced to be burned at the stake – the traditional punishment for a woman guilty of murder. A murmur swept through the crowded hall, considering the harshness and horror of the penalty. Her brother Maurice, the Rufus twins and their fellow ruffians were condemned to be hanged at Tyburn Tree.

'Fank Gawd fer that,' Jack said.

'Mind your language,' Seb told him.

Now the mayor was in no mood to be lenient to those who had betrayed their high offices and the authority the city had bestowed upon them but the rest of the miscreants were still men of standing. Hanging was not for them.

'John Stocker, Paul Draper and Thomas Rigby.' The Mayor glared down at the three men like the Almighty Himself from the height of the judgement bench. 'You each lose your position of authority, never to hold public office of any kind ever again. You will be detained and imprisoned in the gaol at Ludgate until such time as you have each paid the sum of one hundred marks sterling as a fine.'

'That's ridiculous!' Stocker protested, 'I don't have such money as that.'

'Silence!' roared the mayor. 'Then, because I take a vehement aversion to men who abuse the advantage of their high office, with the sanction of King Edward, you will all be exiled, not only from our gracious city but from this blessed realm of England for the rest of your lives. Your betrayal of the trust of your fellow citizens makes you no longer fit to tread upon English soil. You offend my sight.' The mayor turned to the sergeants-at-arms. 'Take them away.'

'Well, at least the devils will be hanged by their bloody purse-strings,' Jude said as left the Guildhall. 'The city coffers will feel the benefit. Marjory has her revenge and Lawrence's soul has been saved from eternal damnation. So why is it, little brother, that you look like a horse just pissed on your best boots, eh?'

'It doesn't seem right to me that a woman and those lesser fellows pay with their lives for a crime in which the instigators, being of higher status, are punished only with payment of fines.'

'What would be the point of fining those who have no money anyway?' Jude said, 'And they have to be made to pay something and their miserable bloody lives are all that they can forfeit. Stands to reason, Seb.'

'Aye. I suppose you be correct. I only hope that Alice At-Bowe's sentence is commuted to hanging. The thought of burning her chills my blood.'

The following morning, Lawrence Ducket's body – no longer that of a suicide – was retrieved from the ditch. Shrouded in finest woollen cloth, the goldsmith's earthly remains were accorded all the proper funeral rites that were his due and given Christian burial by the Grey Friars. A goodly crowd accompanied his body upon its final brief journey, along with Marjory, family and friends, Seb and Jude and even the disgruntled priest, Father Simon Thornbury, from St Mary-le-Bow. In his will, Lawrence had said he wanted to lie in St Mary's, it being his parish church and the place where his parents had their fine brass images set in the floor. But it was not to be. Defiled and sullied, the church was being boarded up, it parishioners forced to worship elsewhere, until Bishop Kemp should re-consecrate and sanctify it anew.

After the funeral, Seb had one more obligation. He went to Budge Row to visit Ralph Aldgate, the victim of the mishap that had set this tragedy in motion. Surgeon Dagvyle was at Ralph's house, changing the linen bindings that swathed the man's head. Ralph was propped up on a mound of pillows, looking pale as a wax candle but, as the surgeon had foreseen, he was not dying of his injury after all.

'This is Master Sebastian Foxley,' Dagvyle introduced Seb to the invalid. 'He sent for me after your accident. He probably saved your life.'

'Accident! Not from what others have told me.' Ralph Aldgate's voice was rasping. Dagvyle offered him a cup of water that was waved away.

'How are you feeling, sir?' Seb asked, coming a little closer to the bed.

'Bad. What do you expect? I have a head wound I am like to die of, no thanks to you.'

'To me? I protest, sir. The fault was not mine.'

Dagvyle intervened.

'You should be grateful to Master Foxley. Thus far, he has paid your medical bills but no longer, if he has any sense.'

'Don't lecture me, surgeon, I'm a sick man upon my death bed.'

'No, you are not. True, you may be abed for some weeks but 'tis not your death bed, I assure you.'

'I merely came to wish you a swift recovery,' Seb said, already backing towards the door.

'There will be naught swift about it. I shall most likely be bedridden for life.' Despite his words, Ralph Aldgate was sufficiently roused to anger to be half out of bed already.

'Forgive me. I should not have come,' Seb said. 'I meant only to make a gesture of neighbourly concern but I see I was mistaken. Good day to you, sir.'

'And good riddance! Get out and don't bother me again.' It seemed the fellow's injuries in no way prevented his shouting loud enough for the entire street to hear him. 'You're not welcome here.'

It was many months before Ralph Aldgate made a complete recovery but his troubles were not over yet. In his wisdom, the bishop saw fit to try Ralph in the ecclesiastical court – the fellow being a cleric – on a charge of conspiracy, aiding and abetting in the murder of Lawrence Ducket. Surgeon Dagvyle's testimony that Ralph was utterly senseless, witless and incapable of aught but drawing breath at the time saved him but, just like those who had wrought vengeance on his behalf, he too was fined to excess. Some thought it was more a case of punishment for consorting with the likes of Alice At-Bowe than anything else. Marjory Ducket for one believed it to be more than justified.

Jack had had his brief moment of fame which couldn't end too quickly for his peace of mind.

He still suffered nightmares until the sheriff, the under-sheriff and the beadle were shipped to other lands. Only then could the lad sleep easy, knowing the fellows wouldn't be coming for him in the night hours, when the darkness was the colour of betrayal.

Author's Note

Much of this tale is based on a true story. In November 1284, a London goldsmith, Lawrence Duket [the original spelling], did have a fight with the Town Clerk, Ralph of Aldgate, over a woman, Alice Atte-Bowe, with these same consequences. The sheriff of the day, Jordan Godchepe, together with 'other citizens of note' but unnamed, violated the sanctuary of St Mary-le-Bow church with Alice and 'fifteen ruffians' and hanged Duket, making it appear that he had committed suicide. Duket's body was flung in a ditch to rot. But there was indeed a young lad who witnessed everything and told his story, eventually, at a royal inquest. Of course, it wasn't our Jack.

The Foxleys were not involved either and nothing is recorded of Duket's family, if he had one. Neither did the incident occur at Christmas but a writer of fiction is allowed to take liberties and the merry traditions of a medieval Christmastide made a good contrast with the gruesome happenings. My only addition to the outcomes was to have the sheriff and notable citizens exiled as well as 'hanged by the purse'. History doesn't say what became of the lad who bore witness against such important people but he must have spent the rest of his life – whether short or long – looking over his shoulder. So I've sent them abroad. Our Jack has too many other things to do in future Foxley adventures to spend time worrying about Sheriff Stocker and company.

My thanks go to the Editor for pointing out some details concerning medieval organs:

A portative organ would have been a hand held organ with 12 notes, so no middle C and A, just an octave and a bit. A positive organ would have had about 4 octaves and sounds more like the one described in the story here. Both were popular between the 12th and 15th centuries.

Toni Mount

Toni Mount earned her research Masters degree from the University of Kent in 2009 through study of a medieval medical manuscript held at the Wellcome Library in London. Recently she also completed a Diploma in Literature and Creative Writing with the Open University.

Toni has published many non-fiction books, but always wanted to write a medieval thriller, and her novels *"The Colour of Poison"*, *"The Colour of Gold"*, *"The Colour of Cold Blood"* and now *"The Colour of Betrayal"* are the result.

Toni regularly speaks at venues throughout the UK and is the author of several online courses available at www.medievalcourses.com.

Toni Mount

The Fifth
Sebastian Foxley
Medieval
Murder Mystery

The Colour of Murder

Prologue

HE CHAMBER beneath the Palace of Westminster was cobweb-draped and thick with the dust of centuries. Few knew of its existence now but these two. The air was dry and chill as the grave. Nameless things had lived and died in this stone vault. They had discovered it a decade before; a place where their late and much-mourned mother had been able to practise undisturbed. A single torch lit the gloom, the light unable to penetrate the arched recesses of this forgotten room but enough to show an open book lying on a table.

He stoked the little brazier to life; she placed a copper dish above the flames to heat a precise measure of rain water.

'This will work, won't it, sister?' he asked, touching her hand in an intimate gesture.

'Have faith. 'Tis our mother's own instructions that we follow. What she has written in the grimoire has never failed us before and will not do so now.' The woman consulted the parchment pages of the book. Murmuring ancient incantations as the water began to boil, she took a handful of leaves from a linen bag. Lance-shaped and rough to the touch, they were dried and crumbled readily as she sprinkled them into the bubbling dish. 'In the name of the Dark Lord and his mistress, Hecate the Wise Woman, I stir this brew thrice widdershins.' She took up an elder rod in her left hand and gently set the water turning in the opposite direction to that which the sun travels by day and the moon and stars by night. An earthy smell arose from the steam. The brazier flames reflected off her silken sleeve as she moved the rod, and glinted on her pale hair, turning it to molten gold.

'Is a single handful sufficient for the task?' he asked. They both knew there could be no mistake in this matter. The future safety, prosperity and happiness of all their family depended upon the efficacy of this potion. 'A few more leaves cannot help but make certain.'

'Be silent, brother. I know what I am about. Our mother taught me well. The leaves of the foxglove are potent indeed. There is enough in this dish to over-try the hearts of my lord husband and all his kin, if we wish to. But for now one brother will suffice. We cannot afford to attract notice with a sudden rush of dead Plantagenets.'

They both laughed, knowing that time would come.

'No. You are right, sister. I fear I am over anxious about this. So much depends...'

She pressed her fingertips to his lips.

'...Depends upon silence, dearest brother. Now we let the potion infuse until it be cooled, then you may decant it into the wine cask. Be sure to wash your hands after. Now, I must leave you. Edward will require my presence when he greets the French ambassador and I am hardly dressed to play my part.'

'Sister, you are a veritable queen whatever your attire. Go then. Dazzle the fools.'

At the foot of the stair she paused and turned, retracing her steps to kiss him fervently.

'Be careful, brother. May the Dark Lord oversee all our endeavours.' She smiled and he returned that smile, confident now that all would be well.

Chapter 1

Thursday, the twelfth day of February, 1478
The Palace of Westminster

RICHARD, DUKE of Gloucester, had been summoned by his brother, King Edward, for a private audience so the presence of others was unexpected. More worrying was the number of the queen's relatives in attendance and particularly so since he wished to beg a favour of Edward – one he believed the king would be more likely to grant, if they were alone.

Richard removed his fur-trimmed hat and bent the knee before his sovereign as etiquette required, even of a prince of royal blood.

'Up, up, little brother,' said the king, waving Richard to his feet. 'Today should be yet another occasion to please you immensely.' Edward was lounging on a padded chair by the blazing hearth, his feet upon a velvet foot stool.

'Indeed, sire? I thought this was to be a privy audience?'

'And so it is, Dickon, but witnesses will be required.'

'Witnesses?' Richard began toying with his finger ring, a nervous habit of his. Realising what he was doing, he clasped his hands behind his back. It did not do to betray his feelings before the queen's brother, Anthony Woodville, Earl Rivers, nor her sons from her first marriage.

Anthony Woodville stood behind the king's right shoulder, as close as he dared without hindering the movement of the royal arm in raising the wine cup to the royal lips. Impeccably attired in the latest – and to Richard's mind – absurd fashion, the earl's voluminous black sleeves flared from the elbow and almost swept the floor. His pale hair, hanging to his shoulders, was perfectly groomed and trimmed; his pointed chin close-shaven. Some exotic scent wafted in the duke's direction each time the earl gestured with his arms, which was often enough to become irritating. To be truthful, Richard found Lord Anthony irritating in any case; his very presence an annoyance.

As for the queen's sons by her first husband, Thomas and Richard Grey, at a year or two younger than himself, they had made his time at court a misery in his youth, teasing him for his lack of knowledge of courtly ways and who was who. In truth, they had mocked and bullied him as a bumpkin from the shires, making him look a fool at every opportunity. He hadn't forgiven nor forgotten a single one of their humiliations. Now they stood to the king's left hand, bold as pike staffs in their silks and satins, be-gemmed and be-feathered like a pair of gaudy trollops. At that moment, naught would have pleased him more than to slap the smirks from their cunning faces. But retribution would have to wait. Richard could be the most patient of men, when necessary.

The king clicked his fingers and Anthony Woodville handed him a rolled parchment. A servant appeared with a portable writing slope; another with pen and ink; a third with a candle, red wax and a lead seal attached to a ribbon.

'You know what this is, Dickon?' The king waved the parchment.

'No, sire. Of course not.' Here he was, forced to show his ignorance before the Woodville-Grey affinity yet again. Why did the king do this to him?

'You will be most gratified to learn, Dickon, that this writ bestows a peerage title upon your little son.'

'But he is barely more than a babe. Naturally, I am delighted, but is he not overly young for such an honour?'

The king looked up from the writing slope, pen poised. His eyes met Richard's and what the duke saw in those ice blue eyes caused the hairs to rise upon the nape of his neck.

'I am creating your little lad Earl of Salisbury.'

'Thank you, sire.' Richard could not even pretend to be pleased. This was no honour. It was a gift of blood for the earldom of Salisbury belonged to their brother George, Duke of Clarence, at present residing at the Tower of London 'at the king's pleasure'. To bestow one of his titles upon another could mean only one thing: George's disgrace was not to be reversed. Or worse? Was Edward sweetening a more bitter pill yet for Richard to swallow? Of a sudden, the duke felt in need of a stool to sit down. Instead, he stepped forward, bent the knee and kissed the coronation ruby on the king's great bear's paw of a hand, then watched as 'Edwardus Rex' was scribbled at the foot of the parchment before it passed to the servant, standing ready with the sand-shaker, to dry the ink.

Then Anthony Woodville signed his name as a witness and the Grey brothers, each in turn. How appropriate, Richard thought, that those who so greatly desired George's downfall should sign away what was rightfully his to another. How long would it be before they contrived a similar fate for himself? The heavy seal was affixed by means of a blob of red wax to attach the ribbon and when the wax had set, Edward presented the parchment to Richard.

'When your lad is older, he will be required to do homage to me for the title, of course. Until then, you can enjoy all the revenues and estates it entails.' Edward's smile might have seemed genuine enough to those who knew him less well but Richard recognised it for what it was: a cold, calculated curving of the lips – a warning he understood.

'My lord,' Richard began, 'Edward, by your leave, I would speak with you alone.'

'I'm a busy man, little brother...'

'As I realise, sire, but this is of the utmost importance to us both. I ask permission to visit George at the Tower. He must be so...'

The king, never one for rapid movement, shot from his chair like a man scalded and grabbed Richard's arm in a painful grip.

'No!' he roared. 'I utterly forbid it.'

'But I...'

'I said no. Let that be an end to it.'

Richard was wincing, his upper arm in agony.

'I merely want...'

The king shook him violently.

'You go near him, write to him...' Spittle sprayed with the king's every word. His face was puce with anger. 'You have communication with him in any way whatsoever and I swear, Dickon, you'll find yourself likewise, in the Tower, locked away indefinitely. Do I make myself quite clear on this matter?'

'Aye.'

'What?'

'You do, your grace.' Richard cleared his throat. 'You make yourself perfectly clear, sire.'

The king flung his brother loose from his grasp like a discarded rag.

'You defy me on this, you'll regret the day,' Edward said, turning away, the quiet words more menacing that any blistering tirade.

Belatedly, Richard noticed the faces of Anthony Woodville and the Greys. If looks could slay, he would be a dead man already, three times over. He refused to massage the life back into his throbbing arm while they watched. His humiliation was too great as it was without acknowledging that physical hurt also.

When Gloucester had departed, clutching the royal warrant but having been denied any chance of privy speech with the king, Anthony Woodville stepped over to a side table, strewn with rolls of parchment awaiting the king's attention. Knowing Edward, such attention was unlikely to be forthcoming without someone else's insistence.

Two years older than his brother-in-law, King Edward, Anthony wore his years rather better than his royal relative. Where the king was running to flesh these days, his face heavily jowled and his belly straining his bejewelled belt, Anthony remained lean, his face smooth and unlined, his physique that of a youth half his age of seven-and-thirty. Sober and austere as a monk, he was yet a man of high fashion. The king bedecked himself in damask and velvet of the brightest hues. In contrast, Anthony wore black, in the Burgundian style. Black might seem a sombre colour, true, but its simplicity was all illusion. In truth, it was an excellent way of demonstrating the wearer's wealth and Anthony liked to flaunt the depth of his coffers. Once lavishly scattered with seed pearls and silver thread embroidery, there was naught sombre about such attire.

That's not to say that the queen's brother was a shallow creature much given to show and little else. He was a scholar, a man of letters, a diplomat, a devout pilgrim and a master at the joust, as well as the ultimate courtier.

'I see a certain document here remains unsigned, as yet,' Anthony said, casually moving a parchment roll to the top of the heap. Of course it wasn't signed. The king, poor soul, was encumbered with a conscience, albeit one that might absent itself on occasion, when convenient. But George's death warrant went far beyond convenience. Clarence's death was a matter of survival for the Woodvilles.

The Foxley house in Paternoster Row, London

Everyone seemed cheerful enough in the workshop this morn. Jude Foxley had arrived – promptly for once – from his lodgings with Dame Ellen in Cheapside, kissed his betrothed, Mistress Rose, tenderly upon the lips for a good few minutes before settling himself at the binding table where collated pages awaited stitching. Feeling pleased with life, at least for the moment, he was whistling a lively tune. Rose could usually be relied upon to improve his erratic humours.

Taking his cue from Jude, Tom Bowen was grinning as he copied out a passage from the exemplar propped on its stand, enjoying the way his quill formed the letters, smelling the acidic tang of the ink as it flowed. Kate Verney, their new apprentice, was practising her letters at the desk opposite.

'Watch the way you finish the letters, lass,' Tom advised her, 'Else the ink will run into a tail. Hold the quill a little more upright. That's better.' It wasn't so long since Tom had been having the same difficulty but now he was coming to the end of his apprenticeship. One more year and he would be a journeyman, paid a daily wage, but he was good enough already to work without constant supervision from Master Seb.

Kate rewarded his help with one of her bright, gleeful smiles and he thought how much more pleasant she was than her predecessor, Jack Tabor. Not that Jack was gone; just that he was no longer trying to learn the stationer's and illuminator's craft. A lad who couldn't learn his letters, he had discovered a talent for carving in wood. He was content now – or as content as a moody fourteen-year-old could be – fashioning fine book covers for the Foxley workshop, paid a small wage with bed and board thrown in. It was better for all concerned.

Rose sat by the workshop door, ready in case any customers came in. It was a fact that she drew men like a lodestone drew iron, her pretty face and comely shape attracting admirers to the shop and they just might be tempted to commission or buy the Foxleys' wares while they were busy gawping at her. In the meantime, she deftly cut and shaped goose feather quills, ready for use. She was a fair scribe herself, though with little training. As the daughter of a glover, Rose was neat, careful and skilful in whatever she undertook. Her glance kept straying to Jude, busy stitching folios with his back to her. Nevertheless, every glance lit the light of love in her eye and brought a blush to her cheek.

There should have been light and laughter in the kitchen too. Sebastian Foxley, master of the house, sat at the board with his wife, Mistress Emily.

'I've been so longing to tell you, Seb, but it was never the right moment. We were never alone,' Emily said. 'I thought you might have guessed anyway by now, seeing I'm plumper already.'

'Aye, of course I, er, noticed, Em,' Seb lied, feeling guilty for having noticed naught of the kind. If a saint in a Book of Hours had grown a little fatter, he would have seen the change straightway.

'You are pleased, aren't you, Seb?'

'I-I'm shocked, Em. In truth, I thought we might never have children. Are you quite certain? There is no doubt?'

'How many times do I have to say it? Shall I put it in writing for you? Perhaps then you'll believe me. I AM WITH CHILD, husband. I can make it no plainer than that. You are happy about it, aren't you? I might almost think you don't want to become a father.'

'The thought of fatherhood pleases me b-but 'tis a dangerous thing for a woman: childbirth. I be afraid for your health, Em, is all. I love you, so I worry for you. You cannot blame me for being concerned.'

'You don't want our child! I can tell. Well, too bad. A child is coming whether you like it or not, Sebastian.' With that, the tears came and Emily turned to flee up the wooden stairs to their bedchamber and slammed the door after, causing a shower of dust to drift down from the ceiling.

Seb sighed and shut his eyes tight, like one in dreadful pain. He felt close to weeping himself. This was the most fearful thing, the possibility he had been secretly dreading ever since their wedding day almost two and a half years before. As the months went by without any sign, he had begun to hope it was never going to happen but now the worst had come to pass after all and there was naught he could do. He was a fool. He should have told Em the truth afore they were wed and now it was far too late.

The morning was wearing on yet Seb hadn't come into the workshop. More to the point, Jude thought, no ale jug and cups had come either. Earlier, there had been raised voices in the kitchen and Jude decided it was time to discover why no mid-morning ale had been served. And why his brother had done not one iota of work. He found Seb slumped at the board, brooding. His face was pale as ashes; not that he was ever rosy cheeked.

'What are you doing, Seb? Are you sick, or something?'

'No, Jude, nothing like that.'

'I heard the argument. What was that about, eh? You want some ale?'

'Got some, thanks.' Seb's head bowed lower, such that his fine hair hung like a dark curtain, hiding his face from view. It was a pose employed to conceal feelings he knew his eyes would betray.

'Just as well; there's hardly any left in the jug.'

'Have mine.' Seb pushed his full cup towards Jude.

'You don't want it? What's amiss then? Em take you to task for snoring last eve?'

'No 'tis worse than that.'

'Farting then?'

'This is serious, Jude.'

'Oh lord, you couldn't manage to get it up when she wanted. That's bloody serious indeed.'

'I *can* manage it and that's the problem,' Seb cried. 'That's the whole problem, don't you see: Em is with child!'

There was a long pause as Jude took in the news.

'So? That's good, isn't it? Make an uncle of me, mm?'

'I am scared, Jude. Supposing the babe takes after me? You remember what our Pa said: birthing me, all twisted and misshapen, killed our mother. What if that happens to Em? I couldn't live with it. I certainly couldn't do what our Pa did: forgiving me for killing the woman he loved and treating me so kindly all those years. Unlike Pa, I'm no saint.'

'Mm. I see your difficulty.'

'What am I going to do, Jude? Should I tell Em about... about w-what I did to our mother, do you think? I don't want to scare her, but... Do you think she ought to know?'

Jude blew out his breath; took a hefty swig of ale.

'I suppose there's no doubt but it's yours?' he asked over the rim of the cup.

'What? What are you saying? You think Em's been with some other? No, not that. Not Em.'

Jude shrugged.

'Well, I don't know. Tell me honestly, little brother, are you capable of-of siring a babe? There. I've said it. I always wondered when you wed, if you'd be able to, seeing the way you were before.'

'Em has never complained.'

'So, I suppose there's no way of knowing, unless you ask her.'

'Ask her what?'

'If the babe is yours. It's not so long ago that she was heartsick for Gabriel Widowson, is it?'

'Jude! It's mine, I tell you.'

'It would be easier if it wasn't. Then you need have no fear for the outcome.'

'For pity's sake, will you stop this!' Seb thumped the board with clenched fists, making the ale cup jump. 'Everything's going to Hell in a hand-basket and there's naught I can do. I just want peace and quiet. Can I not have that in my own house?'

'Don't take on so,' Jude said, putting an arm around his brother's narrow shoulders, only to be shrugged off.

'Leave me alone.'

'Have it your way then. Just don't forget that the 'Sir Gawain and the Green Knight' manuscript needs to be finished, so the customer may approve it and choose a binding for it and – most important, little brother – you're supposed to be at Crosby Place after dinner.'

'Oh, dear God aid me,' Seb groaned, burying his face in his ink-stained hands – the badge of his craft. 'I cannot face Duke Richard, not this day.'

'Just think of the bloody money, Seb. You'll need his lordship's coin more than ever with an extra mouth to feed.'

The Duke of Gloucester's residence of Crosby Place, Bishopsgate, in the City of London

This afternoon, Seb was to make the preliminary sketches for a portrait, to determine the most advantageous and complimentary pose for his noble subject. He awaited the Duke of Gloucester in the magnificent solar, where the oriel window, facing to the south-east, let in as much light as possible, that the ladies might see to do their fine embroideries or read. It also gave a view over the gardens, verdant and flower-spangled in summer but now gaunt and colourless except for the yellow catkins dancing on the hazel trees. Not much else showed any promise of spring as yet.

Lord Richard came from his closet that opened off the solar, leaving the door wide open. Within the little room, Seb could see a carven prie-dieu with a dark velvet cushion to spare the duke's knees as he prayed. The indentations were deep and well-worn – a good deal of praying must have gone on there of late. The prie-dieu was set before a little altar with a crucifix on the wall above and a pair of slender bees-wax candles still burning. The candlelight glinted on the gold leaf of a triptych – the one Seb had painted for the duke more than two years ago. Those had been troubled times for Seb and Jude and seeing the figures on the wooden panels now, he wondered that he had managed to give them expressions and poses so serene and peaceful. If the work had been commissioned by any person of lesser degree than a royal duke, Seb knew he would probably have abandoned the project, making his sincere apologies at being unable to complete it and returned the money.

'I thought you would be glad to see that your beautiful triptych accompanies me everywhere as I travel, Master Foxley,' the duke said, smiling. 'Not a day passes that I do not gaze upon your exquisite artistry. It looks very well in the candlelight, does it not?'

'It does, your grace, and perhaps such subtle light is kinder to my work than it deserves.'

The duke laughed.

'Your false modesty is not required, master. It looks as good in the starkest light of day. You should be proud of your skills. Now. Shall we to business? How shall you want me to sit?'

As his silver point moved deftly over the prepared paper – a fine line here; a shading there – Seb's grey eyes flickered from subject to drawing, noting the smallest detail. His dark hair, unkempt as usual, fell over his brow as he worked in rapt concentration. He knew the sketches were good. He shifted his legs for better balance, easing that ever-troublesome left hip, leaning against the casement of the oriel window as he worked. The intricacies of his art served well in diverting his thoughts from Emily's condition.

His subject, Lord Richard, sat upright in a cushioned chair, the light playing on his angular profile as clouds scudded across the winter skies beyond the window. He appeared as easy as he ever did; only his hands in his lap – never quite still – betrayed his true state of mind. Seb had his easel set up by the window. The February light was perfect today: bright enough to illuminate his work but not so harsh as to be unkind to Lord Richard's hard chiselled features. They were alone in the chamber, apart from the duke's great wolfhound lying by the fire, sleeping, flicking an ear as he dreamed. What did dogs dream about, Seb wondered, as he traced the curve of the lord's cheek in a single line.

'Sir Robert Percy asked to be remembered to you, Master Sebastian. I should have told you earlier, but it slipped my mind.'

'That is most kind of Sir Robert, I had hoped I might see him here,' Seb replied, smiling at the memory of a good friend.

'Rob did not journey to London with me this time. I gave him leave to remain in Yorkshire with his wife, Joyce. Sadly, she was brought to bed of a still-born bairn a few weeks back and has yet to recover fully.' The duke used the northern word for a babe. 'I grieve for them: they had waited so long for this child. At least Rob has an heir by his first wife, but Joyce's bairn would have been the seal upon their happiness.'

Seb tried to give his entire concentration to sketching a fold in the lord's robe but his blood ran chill, hearing the duke's words.

'Perhaps, your grace would...' he cleared his throat as the words seem to lodge there, '...would kindly pass on my condolences to Sir Robert.'

'Aye, of course. Rob will appreciate them.' The duke glanced at the artist without moving his head. 'And how is your goodwife? You must have been wed for more than two years now. How is the famous May Queen archeress, your beautiful bride?'

'Emily is well, my lord, thank you for enquiring.' Seb wondered at the duke's excellent memory. God knows, he must have a thousand more important things to remember than the May Day revels nigh three years gone and the more recent marriage of a young woman he had met at the time. But of course the man remembered. That was Lord Richard's way: a man with a long and precise memory indeed.

Seb set aside a completed sketch and affixed a fresh sheet of paper to the board with wooden pegs to begin an outline of the duke's head, in profile this time, moving his easel, rather than troubling his subject to get up and summon a servant to shift the heavy chair.

'And your brother? Jude, is his name, if I recall correctly?'

'You do, my lord. Aye, Jude is well but...'

'But?'

'But not as he was. I believe his time in Newgate gaol changed him. He has never been the same since but he has found a good woman of late, God be praised.' Seb drew the details of the gold threadwork collar of the duke's doublet of crimson velvet, fashionably slashed with dove-grey silk. The floor-length robe was of the same luxurious cloth.

'Indeed. Gaol changes any man. I've seen it for myself in my own brother.' Lord Richard sighed heavily and began fidgeting with the ring on his finger.

Seb frowned. It took him a moment to recall that the duke had another brother, apart from King Edward: George, Duke of Clarence, currently lodged in the Tower of London at the king's pleasure. And it seemed the king's pleasure was that he should remain there a long while. Seb didn't know what he could say that wouldn't offend either the king or the duke, so he said nothing. But Lord Richard didn't require a response. His pewter-coloured eyes were focused far beyond the glass of the window, across the rooftops of the city.

'George too is changed,' the duke was saying. 'He, who was so fastidious, now refuses the attentions of his servants and goes unwashed, in soiled linen, beard unshaven, hair uncombed. He hardly eats, claiming his food is likely poisoned, to hasten his end. I saw him last month, briefly, and barely knew him for my own brother. I would attempt to persuade him to allow the servants to tend his needs; urge him to eat. I would beg the king to release him.' Seb saw the duke's shoulders sag beneath the velvet. 'Well, I tried, but now the king has forbidden me to see George again nor even to write to him. And I understand none of it. None of it,' he cried, throwing up his hands.

'I know George has behaved badly in the past,' he continued, 'And the king always forgave him. This time, for some seemingly lesser matter, he is incarcerated. He said the king will have him...' The duke closed his eyes. '...have him executed. I told him that was foolish talk: it will never come to that. And yet...' He shook his head, further disarranging his hair as it lay dark on the gold embroidery but Seb did not remind his sitter to stay still. The poor man was clearly devastated and speaking of things a humble artist had no right to hear, his thoughts with one sibling or the other, in the Tower or at Westminster.

Seb set down his silver point; coughed quietly.

'I have completed the preliminary sketches, my lord. You be free to move now, if you want to. I will just transfer a rough outline to the proper canvas, so you may approve the pose.'

'I apologise. What did you say? My thoughts were far away. Forgive me, Master Sebastian, blathering on.'

'I have near finished for today, sir.'

'Good, good. Shall we meet at an earlier hour come tomorrow: eight of the clock then?'

'Aye, my lord, and I'll bring my apprentice, if I may. I shall start working the pigments, laying in the ground colour, and he will be mixing them for me, if you allow? It will speed the process.'

'Of course. Friday, then. Good day to you, master, and thank you.'

Seb draped a cloth over his easel to protect the work, took up his scrip and bowed out of the duke's presence, well aware he now knew more than he should of high-born folks' affairs.

The Foxley house

That night, after a day fraught with worry, Seb lay abed, staring into the darkness, fretting over Em. No longer occupied with work that might divert his thoughts, every time he closed his eyes, his father's words of long ago tolled like the passing-bell in his ears: 'Your birthing killed your mother'. The news imparted by Lord Richard that Sir Rob's baby had died did not help matters but at least the man's wife survived.

He thought Em was asleep beside him until she asked:

'Why are you so angry about the babe?' He heard the quiver in her voice; knew she had been weeping, silently.

'I'm not.'

'Well, you're not pleased, then.'

'You don't understand. I can't explain.'

'Try.'

'No. Now be quiet and go to sleep, woman. Let me have some peace at this hour.' So he turned his back upon her, leaving her miserable on the far side of the bed. What else could he do?

St Paul's bell chimed the midnight hour. He could not sleep with worry chewing at his soul like this. There was guilt too, for his unkindness to poor Em who had no idea what she had done amiss. Eventually, he left the bed, wrapped his night robe around himself and went quietly downstairs, to endure his wretchedness alone, without disturbing Em.

In the kitchen, the embers of the fire still glowed and he stirred them to life with a poker and added another log from the basket – an extravagance at this time of night but he was desperate for comfort of any kind. He poured a cup of ale and sat at the board with it but did not drink. Tears ran down his face yet he made no effort to wipe them away. Nessie was snoring in the alcove behind the curtain; there was no one to see him weep.

The Colour of Murder is due out Spring 2018

Why not join Toni Mount's mailing list and get a free book PLUS advance information about future books:

www.madeglobal.com/authors/toni-mount/download/

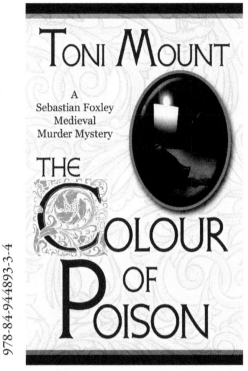

TONI MOUNT

A
Sebastian Foxley
Medieval
Murder Mystery

THE

COLOUR

OF

POISON

978-84-944893-3-4

**The first Sebastian Foxley
Medieval Mystery by Toni Mount.**

The narrow, stinking streets of medieval London can sometimes be a dark place. Burglary, arson, kidnapping and murder are every-day events. The streets even echo with rumours of the mysterious art of alchemy being used to make gold for the King.

Join Seb, a talented but crippled artist, as he is drawn into a web of lies to save his handsome brother from the hangman's rope. Will he find an inner strength in these, the darkest of times, or will events outside his control overwhelm him?

Only one thing is certain - if Seb can't save his brother, nobody can.

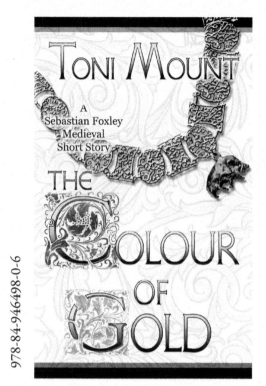

978-84-946498-0-6

The second Sebastian Foxley
Medieval Mystery by Toni Mount.

A wedding in medieval London should be a splendid occasion, especially when a royal guest will be attending the nuptial feast. Yet for the bridegroom, the talented young artist, Sebastian Foxley, his marriage day begins with disaster when the valuable gold livery collar he should wear has gone missing. From the lowliest street urchin to the highest nobility, who could be the thief? Can Seb wed his sweetheart, Emily Appleyard, and save the day despite that young rascal, Jack Tabor, and his dog causing chaos?

Join in the fun at a medieval marriage in this short story that links the first two Sebastian Foxley medieval murder mysteries: *The Colour of Poison* and the full-length novel *The Colour of Cold Blood.*.

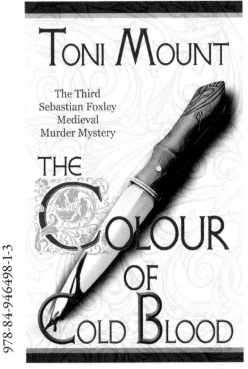

TONI MOUNT

The Third
Sebastian Foxley
Medieval
Murder Mystery

THE COLOUR OF COLD BLOOD

978-84-946498-1-3

**The third Sebastian Foxley
Medieval Mystery by Toni Mount.**

A devilish miasma of murder and heresy lurks in the winter streets of medieval London - someone is slaying women of the night. For Seb Foxley and his brother, Jude, evil and the threat of death come close to home when Gabriel, their well-liked journeyman, is arrested as a heretic and condemned to be burned at the stake.

Amid a tangle of betrayal and deception, Seb tries to uncover the murderer before more women die – will he also defy the church and devise a plan to save Gabriel?

These are dangerous times for the young artist and those he holds dear. Treachery is everywhere, even at his own fireside...

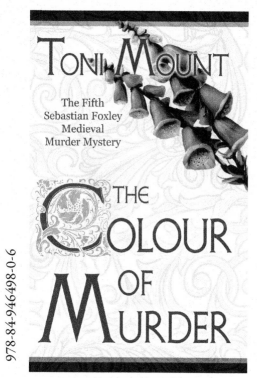

TONI MOUNT

The Fifth
Sebastian Foxley
Medieval
Murder Mystery

THE
COLOUR
OF
MURDER

978-84-946498-0-6

**The fifth Sebastian Foxley
Medieval Mystery by Toni Mount.**

London is not safe for princes or commoners.

In February 1478, a wealthy merchant is killed by an intruder and a royal duke dies at the Tower. Neither case is quite as simple as it seems.

Seb Foxley, an intrepid young artist, finds himself in the darkest of places, fleeing for his life. With foul deeds afoot at the king's court, his wife Emily pregnant and his brother Jude's hope of marrying Rose thwarted, can Seb unearth the secrets which others would prefer to keep hidden?

Join Seb and Jude, their lives in jeopardy in the dangerous streets of the city, as they struggle to solve crimes and keep their business flourishing.

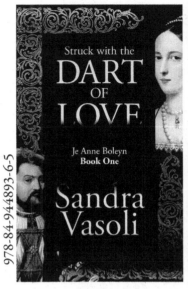
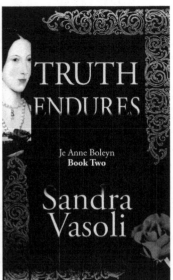

978-84-944893-6-5

978-84-944893-7-2

The *Je Anne Boleyn* series is a gripping account of Anne Boleyn's effort to negotiate her position in the treacherous court of Henry VIII, where every word uttered might pose danger, where absolute loyalty to the King is of critical importance, and in which the sweeping tide of religious reform casts a backdrop of intrigue and peril.

Anne's story begins with *Struck with the Dart of Love*: Tradition tells us that Henry pursued Anne for his mistress and that she resisted, scheming to get the crown and bewitching him with her unattainable allure. Nothing could be further from the truth.

The story continues with *Truth Endures*: Anne is determined to be a loving mother, devoted wife, enlightened spiritual reformer, and a wise, benevolent queen. But others are hoping and praying for her failure. Her status and very life become precarious as people spread downright lies to advance their objectives.

The unforgettable tale of Henry VIII's second wife is recounted in Anne's clear, decisive voice and leads to an unforgettable conclusion...

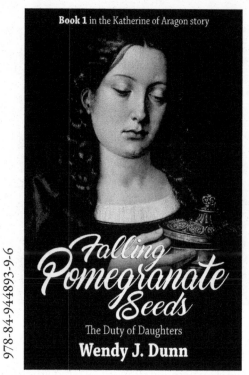

Falling Pomegranate Seeds

The Duty of Daughters

Wendy J. Dunn

978-84-944893-9-6

Book 1 in the Katherine of Aragon Story

Doña Beatriz Galindo.
Respected scholar.
Tutor to royalty.
Friend and advisor to Queen Isabel of Castile.

Beatriz is an uneasy witness to the Holy War of Queen Isabel and her husband, Ferdinand, King of Aragon. A Holy War seeing the Moors pushed out of territories ruled by them for centuries.

The road for women is a hard one. Beatriz must tutor the queen's youngest child, Catalina, and equip her for a very different future life. She must teach her how to survive exile, an existence outside the protection of her mother. She must prepare Catalina to be England's queen.

A tale of mothers and daughters, power, intrigue, death, love, and redemption. In the end, Falling Pomegranate Seeds sings a song of friendship and life.

Why not visit
Sebastian Foxley's web page
to discover more about his
life and times?
www.SebastianFoxley.com

Historical Fiction

Falling Pomegranate Seeds - **Wendy J. Dunn**
Struck With the Dart of Love - **Sandra Vasoli**
Truth Endures - **Sandra Vasoli**
Cor Rotto - **Adrienne Dillard**
The Raven's Widow - **Adrienne Dillard**
The Claimant - **Simon Anderson**

Non Fiction History

Anne Boleyn's Letter from the Tower - **Sandra Vasoli**
Queenship in England - **Conor Byrne**
Katherine Howard - **Conor Byrne**
The Turbulent Crown - **Roland Hui**
Jasper Tudor - **Debra Bayani**
Tudor Places of Great Britain - **Claire Ridgway**
Illustrated Kings and Queens of England - **Claire Ridgway**
A History of the English Monarchy - **Gareth Russell**
The Fall of Anne Boleyn - **Claire Ridgway**
George Boleyn: Tudor Poet, Courtier & Diplomat - **Ridgway & Cherry**
The Anne Boleyn Collection - **Claire Ridgway**
The Anne Boleyn Collection II - **Claire Ridgway**
Two Gentleman Poets at the Court of Henry VIII - **Edmond Bapst**

Children's Books

All about Richard III - **Amy Licence**
All about Henry VII - **Amy Licence**
All about Henry VIII - **Amy Licence**
Tudor Tales William at Hampton Court - **Alan Wybrow**

PLEASE LEAVE A REVIEW

If you enjoyed this book, *please* leave a review at the book seller
where you purchased it. There is no better way to thank the
author and it really does make a huge difference!
Thank you in advance.